7 BILLION LIVES ARE IN DANGER.
13 STRANGERS WITH TERRIFYING NIGHTMARES.
1 ENEMY WILL STOP AT NOTHING TO DESTROY US ALL.

MY NAME IS SAM.
I AM ONE OF THE LAST THIRTEEN.
OUR BATTLE CONTINUES . . .

This one is for Kate Beasley. I hope that one day we are reading her books—JP.

First American Edition 2014
Kane Miller, A Division of EDC Publishing

Text copyright © James Phelan, 2014
Illustrations & design copyright © Scholastic Australia, 2014
Illustrations by Chad Mitchell. Design by Nicole Stofberg

First published by Scholastic Australia Pty Limited in 2014
This edition published under license from Scholastic Australia Pty Limited.

Cover photography: Blueprint © istockphoto.com/Adam Korzekwa; Parkour Tic-Tac © istockphoto.com/Willie B. Thomas; Climbing wall © istockphoto.com/microgen; Leonardo da Vinci (Sepia) © istockphoto.com/pictore; Gears © istockphoto.com/-Oxford-; Mechanical blueprint © istockphoto.com/teekid; Circuit board © istockphoto.com/Bjorn Meyer; Map © istockphoto.com/alengo; Grunge drawing © istockphoto.com/aleksandar velasevic; World map © istockphoto.com/Maksim Pasko; Internet © istockphoto.com/Andrey Prokhorov; Inside clock © istockphoto.com/LdF; Space galaxy © istockphoto.com/Sergii Tsololo; Sunset © istockphoto.com/Joakim Leroy; Blue flare © istockphoto.com/YouraPechkin; Global communication © istockphoto.com/chadive samanthakamani; Earth satellites © istockphoto.com/Alexey Popov; Girl portrait © istockphoto.com/peter zelei; Student & board © istockphoto.com/zhang bo; Young man serious © istockphoto.com/Jacob Wackerhausen; Portrait man © istockphoto.com/Alina Solovyova-Vincent; Sad expression © istockphoto.com/Shelly Perry; Content man © istockphoto.com/drbimages; Pensive man © istockphoto.com/Chuck Schmidt; Black and pink © istockphoto.com/blackwaterimages; Punk Girl © istockphoto.com/Kuzma; Woman escaping © Jose antonio Sanchez reyes/Photos.com; Young woman © Anomen/Photos.com; Explosions © Leigh Prather | Dreamstime.com; Landscape blueprints © Firebrandphotography | Dreamstime.com; Jump over wall © Ammentorp | Dreamstime.com; Mountains, CAN © Akadiusz Iwanicki | Dreamstime.com; Sphinx Bucegi © Adrian Nicolae | Dreamstime.com; Big mountains © Hoptrop | Dreamstime.com; Sunset mountains © Pklimenko | Dreamstime.com; Mountains lake © Janmika | Dreamstime.com; Blue night sky © Mack2happy | Dreamstime.com; Old writing © Empire331 | Dreamstime.com; Young man © Shuen Ho Wang | Dreamstime.com; Abstract cells © Sur | Dreamstime.com; Helicopter © Evren Kalinbacak | Dreamstime.com; Aeroplane © Rgbe | Dreamstime.com; Phrenology illustration © Mcarrel | Dreamstime.com; Abstract interior © Sur | Dreamstime.com; Papyrus © Cebreros | Dreamstime.com; Blue shades © Mohamed Osama | Dreamstime.com; Blue background © Matusciac | Dreamstime.com; Sphinx and Pyramid © Dan Breckwoldt | Dreamstime.com; Blue background2 © Cammeraydave | Dreamstime.com; Abstract shapes © Lisa Mckown | Dreamstime.com; Yellow Field © Simon Greig | Dreamstime.com; Blue background3 © Sergey Skrebnev | Dreamstime.com; Blue eye © Richard Thomas | Dreamstime.com; Abstract landscape © Crazy80frog | Dreamstime.com; Rameses II © Jose I. Soto | Dreamstime.com; Helicopter © Sculpies | Dreamstime.com; Vitruvian man © Cornelius20 | Dreamstime.com; Scarab beetle © Charon | Dreamstime.com; Eye of Horus © Charon | Dreamstime.com; Handsome male portrait © DigitalHand Studio/Shutterstock.com; Teen girl © CREATISTA/Shutterstock.com; Paradise Bay in Antarctica © Maxily | Dreamstime.com; Antactica map © Marcio Silva | Dreamstime.com; Iceberg in the fog, Antarctica © Adeliepenguin | Dreamstime.com; Iceberg with an arch, Antarctica © Adeliepenguin | Dreamstime.com; Antarctica icebergs © Adeliepenguin | Dreamstime.com; Adelie penguins on ice, Antarctic © Adeliepenguin | Dreamstime.com; Ice crevasse © Deborah Benbrook | Dreamstime.com; Iceberg in Antarctica © King Ho Yim | Dreamstime.com; Glacier crevasse © Steven Francis | Dreamstime.com; Blue Ice II © Darryn Schneider | Dreamstime.com; Shipwreck © Totophotos | Dreamstime.com; Shipwreck © Aquanaut4 | Dreamstime.com; Wooden shipwreck © Kennerth Kullman | Dreamstime.com; Old automotive workshop © Mark Soon | Dreamstime.com; Active volcano © Dmitry Pichugin | Dreamstime.com; Volcano eruption, Fimmvorduhals Iceland © Brynjar Gunnarsson | Dreamstime.com; Waiting for a bus in Antarctica © Darryn Schneider | Dreamstime.com; Ice-covered meteorological station © Salajean | Dreamstime.com; An ice-covered meteorological station © Salajean | Dreamstime.com; Radar © Dreamzdesigner | Dreamstime.com; Snowmobile winter landscape © Tyler Olson | Dreamstime.com; Glacier with snowmobile © Tyler Olson | Dreamstime.com; Burning snowmobile © istockphoto.com/stockstudioX ; Antarctica giant blue iceberg floating © istockphoto.com/Grafissimo; Antarctica Lemaire Channel snowy mountain © istockphoto.com/Grafissimo; Ice floe close-up © istockphoto.com/ElsvanderGun.

Internal photography: p38, Tablet © Jbk_photography | Dreamstime.com; p38, Aircraft weather radar © istockphoto.com/olyniteowl; p91, Mud brick wall © istockphoto.com/rcphotos; p91, Cardboard placards © istockphoto.com/imagestock; p125, Tunnel entrance © istockphoto.com/hyslop; p161, GPS handheld device icon © Diana Rich | Dreamstime.com.

Library of Congress Control Number: 2013945972

Printed and bound in the United States of America
1 2 3 4 5 6 7 8 9 10
ISBN: 978-1-61067-282-5

THE LAST THIRTEEN

BOOK TWELVE

JAMES PHELAN

Kane Miller
A DIVISION OF EDC PUBLISHING

PREVIOUSLY

Sam is mourning the loss of Tobias when Eva is revealed as the eleventh Dreamer of the last 13. She has dreamed of her Gear in Australia. The last 13 regroup in London and assure Sam he will lead them to the Dream Gate.

Held captive by pirates, Alex outwits the night watch and the crew take back the ship. As they sail on to Christchurch, Alex dreams of Antarctica. Hans confesses that he believes the Dream Gate itself might be there.

Sam observes a stealth mission to capture Solaris at his deserted island hideout. He is horrified to see the mission go wrong when Solaris ambushes the soldiers and has to witness a terrible massacre of Guardians and Agents.

Eva and Sam leave for Australia, sneaking past the UN security cordon at the Academy. There, they change their plans to alter the future that Eva has dreamed. Eva travels to Uluru with Jabari, the leader of the Egyptian Guardians, while Sam heads north.

In Antarctica, Hans takes Alex on an underwater adventure in a submersible, discovering a wrecked submarine that holds a map. Hiking onward in the snow, Hans and the others fall down a crevasse, forcing Alex to cut the ropes and go on alone. Taking refuge in a thermal cave, Alex uncovers secrets about Antarctica.

Exploring an amazing underground facility beneath Uluru, Eva finds her Gear but is captured by Stella. She shows Eva that her friends, Lora and Xavier, who are trying to shut down a Tesla tower they suspect Stella is using at Chernobyl, have walked into a trap. She orders her men to open fire. Xavier and Lora are the only survivors, rescued by Dr. Dark.

Sam travels to the Wessel Islands where he meets a local Dreamer, Malcolm, who shows him another Dream Universe chamber. Sam's dream there shows him that Eva is still in grave danger so he heads to Uluru with his helicopter pilot, Henk.

After a hair-raising arrival, Sam manages to reach Eva, and together they overcome Stella. As they leave, Solaris appears, but Sam sets off a flood and they flee to safety in the desert. As Henk arrives with Jabari, they are gunned down in a hail of darts, knocking them unconscious . . .

ALEX'S NIGHTMARE

A cursor blinks on the dark screen, bright, flashing. My breath fogs in front of me and I shiver again in the darkness.

"What does it mean?" a voice asks.

I turn away from the computer screen.

Sam stands before me. He's dressed in heavy snow gear, like he's just come through a blizzard. There's a shovel in his hands. He's heaving in deep breaths, like he had to dig his way through endless thick snow to get here.

"Alex," Sam says, "what are you doing? We've been looking everywhere for you."

"Why?"

"The weather's changing fast. There's a super storm coming in, some kind of polar vortex thing. We have to go—now."

"But we haven't gotten what we came for."

"We'll come back tomorrow," Sam says. "We're already a bit snowed in. We're going to have to dig ourselves out. Come on, move!"

I look from Sam to the computer. The cursor still blinks

rhythmically as the file downloads. The screen shows the download is thirty-three percent complete.

I shrug. "I'll stay behind. Come get me tomorrow." I don't look at Sam, I just keep watching the computer. The file I am waiting for is a map of the area, detailed, showing the geography of the vast region. The download via satellite is slow.

Thirty-four percent.

Thirty-five percent.

"Alex, you'll freeze out here—"

"I'll be fine, Sam, really. You go. I'll stay and do this."

Sam is silent.

I sigh and turn around, expecting him to still be standing over me, ready to argue, but he's gone.

"Sam?"

I get up from the chair to follow him. "Sam?" I call out again. "Sam!"

Outside the communications room, I walk down a hall that wraps around in a gentle curve. I find Sam standing by the outside doors with his back to me. He's motionless, facing the doors like he's waiting for something.

"Sam?" I approach him. "Are . . . are you OK?"

There's no answer.

"Sam?"

He swings around, and before I can say anything more, he hits the side of my head with the shovel.

I wake up with a throbbing headache. It feels like my whole face is swollen and on fire. I wince and that makes the pain in my head even worse. I realize everything is moving, ever so slightly, back and forth. And I realize something else—something's not right about what I can see . . .

The world is upside down.

I'm looking at the computer terminal but it's the wrong way up.

I can feel that my ankles are tied together. I can see my wrists are too, dangling uselessly out in front of me. Looking down—*up*—at my feet, I see the rope around my ankles is lashed over a big hook in the ceiling.

I'm hanging from my feet upside down, trussed up like a carcass in a cool room.

Sam comes in.

"Sam!" I say. "What a relief! Help me down from here."

Sam stops next to an old wooden chair. I struggle to recall what happened.

I was working at the computer, downloading something . . . Sam came in and said we had to go and then . . . then what?

My head throbs as Sam begins to drag the chair across the hard concrete floor, the sharp screeching noise knifing into my skull.

The sound stops abruptly, and I wonder why Sam is now in the middle of the room and not next to me, helping me down.

Isn't he dragging the chair over to stand on and cut me free?

He sits down, facing me.

Wha–?

I look at him. We are face-to-face, not far apart, only I am still upside down.

"Alex," Sam says, "this is really simple."

"Sam–what's going on? Why am I tied up?"

"All you have to do is tell me the location." Sam's voice is slow and deliberate.

"The location?" I start to panic. "Of what?"

"Yes. The location." Sam smiles. "Tell me *where* the Gear is. Tell me *that* and we dig our way out of here, together. OK? It really is that simple. Tell me where your Gear is, and we're out of here."

"I–I don't know . . . wait, *my* Gear?"

"Tell me where it is."

"But I don't–"

"Alex, this is important. Don't waste any more time."

What's happening?

"Sam–help me down. This isn't funny, man!"

Sam shakes his head slowly and looks disappointed.

"Sam? What the–? What's going *on?*"

"You tell me," he says.

"Get me down from here," I say through clenched teeth.

"Why would I help you?" Sam replies calmly. "You're not helping me."

"You have to . . . wait—*what did you say?*"

"I need answers, Alex. Tell me where the Gear is."

"I don't *know!*"

"Of course you do. You found it. Tell me."

"I—I didn't! I've never found a Gear!" I struggle against the binds, swaying under the hook that has me hung from the ceiling. "Stop fooling around, Sam! Get me down from here right now, or so help me, when I do get down . . ." The blood is pounding in my ears, my head feels heavy, my skin flushed and hot from hanging upside down.

"When you tell me where—" Sam says evenly.

"I DON'T KNOW!" I scream. "Why are you doing this?! You're supposed to be my *friend!*"

"No," Sam says in a quiet voice, leaning forward. "You're supposed to be *my* friend. It's *you* who's been at the Enterprise all this time, while I was out doing all the hard work. You who has been sailing around in luxury, doing *nothing*, while I've been risking my life. It's *you* who sided with Hans to get the Gear—for him. You're a traitor, Alex. You're working with the enemy. So you can be there at the end? So whatever is beyond the Dream Gate belongs to you, is that it?"

"You're wrong! *Get me down!*"

"Have you been with Hans all this time, down here in Antarctica?"

"Yeah, but . . . '

"But *what*? Wait, let me guess—you were just down here sightseeing?" Sam paces around the room. "Look, Alex, I know you found it. You found the Gear, and you hoped the rest of us would be killed coming to help you, so that you could be there, on your own, at the Gate."

"What? Sam, you're acting crazy. What's with you, man? You know I'd never—"

Sam stops pacing and turns sharply on his heel to face me, eyes fierce. "Tell me where it is, and this can end, OK?"

A muffled explosion sounds from outside, in the distance. Dust drifts down from the ceiling.

"That'd be your friend, Hans," Sam says. "Ticktock, Alex, we don't have much time."

"No—he's not my—I was only with Hans to get this done. To find out what he knows, to help us win."

Sam is silent. I struggle against my wrist binds, the movement rocking me from side to side as I hang there, like a pendulum in motion.

"*You're* the enemy, Alex, when you act like this," Sam says. "Think back. Think back to when you came to Antarctica, wandering across the ice and you found a way into the complex and you found the Gear."

"I, I was . . ." I concentrate.

Faded memories start to swim around my aching head.

I did find it.

"Fire," I whisper, "so much fire. But deep, under a mountain. It's so hot . . ."

"Good," he says, taking a step towards me. "Tell me where you found it. Start there, everything that happened, right up until you got it."

Something's not right. Why's he doing this?

How did I end up here? The shovel! It was HIM!

"I—I can't tell you, Sam," I force myself to say. My eyes widen as the dread fills me, overwhelming me. "All I know is . . . we don't make it, Sam."

At the end, there's only—

Darkness.

SAM

"**A**lex!" Sam sat up in bed, breathless.

The room around him was dark. He felt startled and disoriented.

Where am I?

He got out of bed and looked around.

A hotel room? But how . . . how did I get here?

Sam's head throbbed as he went to the window and looked out.

I'm in a hotel in the middle of a city. But which city?

He switched on the light on the bedside table. A small notepad and pen were placed neatly by the lamp, both imprinted with the hotel's name and location.

I'm in Melbourne. I'm still in Australia.

Eva!

He ran to his hotel door and turned the handle to pull it open, but it was locked. He patted the pockets of his Stealth Suit hoping to feel a room key or swipe card.

Empty.

Sam went to the phone and picked up the receiver.

There was no dial tone. He lifted up the phone base and saw that the cord had been cut.

How'd we get here? We were in the desert, in central Australia. I was going to go back to Uluru, to find the dream chamber hidden beneath it. Eva and I needed to separate—but then what?

He shut his eyes, trying to drown the memories of his recent dream to recall the events before. Then it all came flooding back to him.

The helicopter landed. Henk was there, Jabari was with him.

We were ambushed.

Stella!

Sam looked back at the locked door, all the pieces falling into place now.

We're captive again.

Sam padded quietly over to the door, putting his eye close to the peephole. Three rogue Agents in gray suits stood in the hallway, standing guard.

Great.

Where's Eva? And Jabari and Henk? Are they being held here too?

Sam paced around. He looked out the window. He was at least twenty stories above the city, the glass of the window sealed tight. He searched the room, opening drawers and inspecting the furniture, looking for anything that he could use as a weapon.

When they come in, I'll pretend I'm still asleep . . . taking on three Agents on my own won't be easy, though.

In the bathroom there were small bottles of shampoo and conditioner, a tiny bar of soap, two towels.

Not much use.

He opened the closet. It was empty other than three wooden coat hangers hanging from the rail. He took one, holding it out and practicing a swing with it.

Not quite a baseball bat, but it's better than nothing.

In the quiet of the night, Sam could hear the muffled sounds of movement in the corridor, directly outside his door. He quickly put the pillows under the blanket so that it looked as though he was still in bed, sleeping. He tiptoed to the bathroom, waiting in the darkness.

Sam's heart pounded as he heard the door bleep once with the sound of an electronic key card.

A figure rushed by the bathroom doorway.

Sam jumped out, the coat hanger raised over his head like a club.

"Sam!" Eva said.

Shocked, he turned around. Eva stood in the hallway. The three rogue Agents lay unconscious at her feet.

"You did that?" Sam said to her.

"I did . . . with a *little* help," she said, pointing to Jabari who stood behind Sam, smiling.

"Awesome!" Sam said.

That guy is like some kind of super ninja. How does he do it?

Jabari looked at the wooden coat hanger in Sam's hands. "You were going to club me with that?" he asked.

"Only if you were an Agent, or Stella." Sam grinned. "But where's Henk? We can't leave without him."

Eva's smile faded.

"I'm sorry, Sam," Jabari said. "He's not here. She had no use for your friend. I believe she got rid of him."

"He's *dead?* No!" Sam gasped. "That's not . . . I . . . it's my fault he was ever involved."

"His courage will not be forgotten. But for now, come," Jabari said, leading them out into the hall. "Stella will be close by. It is time to leave."

Sam's watch read 3:21 a.m. They were now across town at a small, beige hotel near the airport.

"I've gotta call Lora, about the next Dreamer," Sam said, almost to himself. He picked up the phone on the desk and was about to press the buttons, but Jabari caught his hand to stop him.

"If you call the Academy from that phone," he said, "there's a very good chance someone from Stella's team will trace the call. They will know by now that we have escaped, but let's not give them any clues to find us. I will try to send a message via this," he said holding up a tablet.

"It's better encrypted and will buy us some time, at the very least."

Eva came over and sat on the edge of the bed next to Sam, yawning away the tiredness. "You've had your dream? Why didn't you say something earlier?" she asked.

"Um, it's a bit complicated this time," Sam said. "This Dreamer doesn't really . . . trust me right now. There was fire, but not from Solaris—it was coming from inside some big cave. A lot of fire . . ." Sam trailed off.

Eva looked confused. "Well, do you know where the next Dreamer is?" she asked. "Or where the cave might be?"

Sam looked up at her, suddenly more alert. "Antarctica. The next Dreamer is there."

"Are you sure? It's just there's not much down there— no one lives there, not full-time, just a bunch of scientists at research stations. It's not really the kind of place you'd just be passing through."

"This Dreamer *is* just passing through, actually. I know he is," Sam said. "It's someone we already know."

"Huh?"

"The next Dreamer is Alex."

"Wow," Eva said, stunned. "That's—that's awesome! I mean, I guess we should have known. What with me being the one before."

"I'm not sure it *is* awesome . . ." Sam interrupted. He stared at the second hand on his watch, ticking away. "The dream was all mixed up. I only caught flashes but

I know we were arguing and somehow Solaris was there, but I couldn't see him. It was so strange. Not like any of the other last 13 dreams I've had. I honestly don't know if Alex will trust me or not."

Jabari looked up from the screen, now paying closer attention to what Sam was saying.

"Of course he does," Eva said. "Why wouldn't he?"

"I'm not sure. But in my dream, we were working against each other."

"But—how? *Why?*"

"Because," Sam said, looking at his friend, "I think Alex has sided with Hans."

An hour later, they all left the hotel, sneaking out through a rear fire exit and hurrying across the deserted parking lot.

The predawn air was warm and planes roared over-head, taking off from runways nearby. Sam and Eva had their backpacks slung over their shoulders, and they followed close behind Jabari, who was striding across the street and flagging down a taxi.

"So instead of being picked up in the morning as planned," Eva said, "we're going to get on a plane ourselves and meet Lora on the way to Antarctica?"

Jabari nodded. "Yes," he said. "We are booked on the

first flight south. We will be leaving in just over an hour from now."

"But shouldn't we regroup?" Eva said, looking at Jabari. "Wait for reinforcements if Stella is after us? Arrive in Antarctica with a whole army?"

"When we land in Hobart, we will be meeting Lora, and whichever Guardians did not go to Chernobyl," Jabari said wearily. "It's not much of an army, I'm afraid, but we don't have any other choice."

"But if they are coming from the other side of the world, we'll be waiting too long—Stella will find us before Lora does," Sam said, concerned.

"Lora is traveling on the Enterprise jet—she will arrive not long after us. We head to Alex together."

"Thing is," Sam said, still frowning, "it still might be too late. I didn't see Alex with his Gear in my dream, but that doesn't mean he didn't dream of it. Even if we have the same dream, the Dreamers sometimes see details I don't and vice versa. If Alex now thinks of me as an enemy, like we were in the dream, and tells Hans about it, then the Gear will be lost to us."

"If we have any hope of convincing Alex of the truth, we have to get to him as soon as possible," Jabari said.

Sam nodded.

"Sam," Eva said quietly, looking out at the twinkling lights of the airport from the taxi, "we know that somehow Solaris has been spying on your dreams . . ."

Sam nodded as he stared out the window. "I know," he said. "Another reason we have to get to Alex as fast as we can. Besides, the clock is ticking. We don't have many days left to fulfill the prophecy."

ALEX

"**A**rgh!" Alex screamed as he woke, panicking, not knowing where he was. His hand reached out, fumbling to find the flashlight by his side.

Oh—that's right, now I remember. I'm lost, in a cave, in Antarctica, with hardly any food.

Great.

Alex sat up and ate the last of his energy bars. He was huddled inside the snow cave, with nothing but the food and drink still left in his backpack. Tucked into a pocket of his snowsuit was his emergency GPS transponder.

My dream of Sam . . . he wanted a Gear. But I didn't see, I don't remember finding it.

What if he doesn't believe me in real life, like in the dream?

Alex turned the thought over anxiously in his head. He knew that his mother, Phoebe, understood what he was doing here in Antarctica with Hans. But what if, after everything that he'd been through on the long voyage here, the others didn't really believe his motives? The thought had never even occurred to Alex before.

They wouldn't really think I would join one of our enemies . . . would they?

Alex had a suspicion there was something else in the dream, something about Sam, or maybe Solaris. He shook his head to clear his thoughts. Whatever it was, there was a mental block there now.

He stood up and used his flashlight to inspect the scene once more. Water dripped from the ceiling and he constantly had to wipe his face free from condensation. It wasn't that cold. In fact, the thermal pool outside the cave made it slightly warm. Steam rose in the frozen air, carried into the cave and condensed inside, forming a natural steam chamber that, at the far end, was so warm he'd stripped down to his thermals in the night and slept on his snowsuit like a mattress. Every now and then there'd be a loud plop as the steam collected on the ceiling and dripped into the center of the pool.

The hypnotic sound of the rhythmic dripping calmed Alex slightly, and it was only then that he realized the real significance of his dream.

But maybe it's true. I am one of the last 13.

His mouth fell open in amazement as he tried to process the impossibility of the situation.

Think, Alex! C'mon, you have to get out of this. Everyone is depending on you. If you fail, they will believe the dream—they will believe you're a traitor.

And what about the prophecy? I have to survive—the fate of the world depends on it!

Alex paced in the cave, gathering his thoughts. His eyes strayed to the rock under his feet.

Even the floor isn't just snow and ice.

Huge sections of the stone were covered with intricate carvings, far grander and more detailed than any Roman or Greek mosaic he'd seen in his history books at school. As he shone his flashlight over a wider arc on the floor, Alex could see delicate depictions of starry skies that were crisscrossed with lines of the zodiac. Below them was extravagant scenery of people, animals and a landscape filled with palm trees.

Alex looked closer at the impressive mosaic sky, counting in his head.

This shows the thirteen zodiac signs that Ahmed told me about.

He traced the constellations with his fingers.

There!

Ophiuchus . . . we meet again.

But the most intriguing—and incredible—part of the scene before him were the structures that dotted the huge image etched into the stone floor. These structures, with tiny figures of people congregated around them, were unmistakable.

Pyramids.

"I gotta get to the others, tell them about this."

Alex dressed, pulling on his heavy snow boots and snowsuit.

Maybe if I reach higher ground, get out of this valley and climb one of the mountains, I can set off the GPS transponder. Then I just gotta hope the signal gets picked up.

Piece of cake.

"Oh man, imagine some cake right now." Alex's stomach rumbled at the thought.

OK, that seems like a good plan to start with.

It felt good to have a plan—the thought of doing something took his mind off his hunger and the fact that he was stuck on the most hostile continent on the planet.

Alex inspected the entire cave, looking over every detail of the engraving, every tiny etching, being careful not to miss anything that might be connected to the last 13 or the race. As he was searching in the silence, several thoughts kept looping in his mind, refusing to leave him alone.

I'm one of the last 13.

Where's my Gear?

Why didn't Sam believe me?

04

SAM

"Hey . . ." Eva said from her window seat, nudging Sam who sat between her and Jabari. "Look. We're almost there."

"Great," Sam said, looking out at the view of the Tasmanian landscape below. During the hour flight to Hobart, he kept quiet with his own thoughts. The morning outside looked gray.

"I saw you napping before," Sam said to her.

"I was just closing my eyes," Eva replied.

"You were snoring."

"Fine, I slept a tiny bit."

"Did you dream?" Sam asked.

"Yeah," Eva said, a slight smile on her face as she reminisced. "An old dream though, of my family. Christmas, actually."

Sam smiled. "I love those dreams."

"Yeah," Eva said. "Me too."

"Ever wish this never happened?" Sam asked. "That our dreams were good or bad, nothing more?"

Eva nodded.

"Me too," Sam said.

Sam looked past Eva out the window, and soon felt the plane bank slightly, dropping speed and then touching down bumpily on the tarmac. The aircraft taxied to the passenger terminal. He got up and followed Jabari and Eva out.

As he walked through the small airport, he felt a strange feeling brewing in the pit of his stomach. He knew that this time it was not just about a race to the next Dreamer, or the next Gear.

It's a battle to survive . . . and maybe, worst of all, a battle for Alex.

And in the loneliest place on Earth.

As they waited for Lora to arrive, Sam and Eva talked in hushed tones about the race, the others back in London and what might happen next. Jabari sat nearby, constantly scouring the terminal with alert eyes.

The man never rests.

"Well, I know the prophecy said—" Sam was saying.

"Lora!" Eva interrupted, jumping up and running across the terminal, threading through passengers to find Lora who walked quickly towards them. She gave her a hug.

Lora came up to Sam and Jabari, greeting them and introducing the two tall Guardians with her.

They all went over to a cafe that had just opened up for breakfast.

"Bad news. Jedi has tracked Stella's movements," Lora said to them. "She was just seen at the Melbourne airport."

"Where's she headed?" Jabari asked.

"We'll know soon, I've got a Guardian watching them," Lora replied. "You guys were very lucky to escape at the hotel."

"Jabari got us out," Sam said.

"It was nothing," Jabari said, smirking. "Almost too easy."

Lora returned a small smile, but still looked worried.

Eva showed Lora the tiny Gear from Australia that she still wore inconspicuously around her neck.

"Well done, all of you," Lora said, smiling wider this time as she admired the twin brass disks that caught the light as Eva held them up. "We're getting so near to the end now."

"Yeah, and it was another close call," Sam said.

"You guys did good, Sam," Lora said. "You survived."

Everyone was silent at the table, clearly thinking about the horrific ambush in Chernobyl that Lora had only just escaped herself.

"I will check the arrangements for our transport south," Jabari said, breaking the uncomfortable silence and excusing himself from the group.

"How are the others?" Sam asked Lora.

"OK," Lora said. "After Tobias, and the events at Solaris'

hideout and Chernobyl . . . they're as good as they can be, I guess. No one thought this would be easy."

Sam nodded. Then he saw Lora and Eva smile.

"What?" he said. "What is it?"

Sam sensed a presence behind him, but before he could turn around, hands covered his eyes.

"Guess who?"

"Ha!" Sam said, recognizing the Italian accent. "Gabriella!"

"No!"

"Huh?" Sam turned. Gabriella was there, but it was Arianna who had her hands over Sam's eyes. "What are you guys doing here?"

"With our reduced man power, we brought Arianna and Gabriella to help out with our task ahead," Lora explained. "Strictly no field work though—"

She looked at Gabriella and Arianna meaningfully, and Sam wondered if this had been a point of debate on the flight here.

"We'll be the communications experts," Arianna said to Sam.

"While you are looking for the Gear, we will be holding the fort, this is how to say it, yes?" Gabriella added.

Lora nodded. "Antarctica is notoriously unreliable for satellite and phone connections. We will have Gabriella and Arianna with Eva at the base to keep us in contact with Jedi, the Professor and the director."

"What?" Eva exclaimed. "I have to stay there too?"

"Eva, you've been in enough danger recently. It makes no sense to have you out in the field unless you really need to be. Sam needs to find the Dreamer, and the Gear."

"OK, I guess," Eva said, begrudgingly. "When do we head for Antarctica?"

"They're readying the jet now, refueling and doing flight plans," Lora replied. "We've got another two Guardians and two Agents with us. They're organizing supplies for us. We'll leave as soon as they return."

"Where do you get supplies for an Antarctic expedition at such short notice?" Eva asked. "Wait, why am I even asking? They're buying stuff from the Save The World store, right?"

"You'd be surprised," Lora said with a grin.

XAVIER

"**S**eriously, there's nothing to worry about," Xavier whispered to Maria as they followed the rest of the last 13 into the Professor's office. "It's not like we're in trouble. Remember, we're the good guys."

"I want you all to pack," the Professor said to them, "and to be ready to leave the country."

Maria looked at Xavier with a questioning look.

"Leave the country?" Rapha repeated.

"Yes," the Professor replied. "After dinner tonight, you will all leave here—under the radar, of course."

Xavier nodded. Looking around at his last 13 companions assembled in the Professor's office, he knew Maria was anxious. She'd been having bad dreams all week, just like he had. Cody seemed calm. Rapha was nodding, thinking about what was ahead. Issey still seemed half asleep. Zara looked nervously at the other faces in the room. Poh was smiling and gave Xavier a thumbs-up as he caught his eye. Xavier grinned in return.

He looked out the windows. The view was familiar now—the UN security cordon remained, circling the perimeter of the campus. There'd been no further security breaches at the Academy and it almost seemed like the UN guards were there mainly to keep the world's media at a distance. The interest in the last 13, and the fate of the world, had unsurprisingly not diminished in the slightest. If anything, it had only grown in intensity. More news choppers circled the sky, skirting the no-fly zone established over the campus grounds.

"You will be leaving with Phoebe," the Professor explained further. "Under the cover of darkness, you'll slip through the cordon outside."

"But I thought we needed to stay here, together, for the race?" Xavier asked.

The Professor nodded his head. "Yes, that is true. But I have decided, in consultation with Lora and the director of course, that the Academy might not be the best place for you at this point." The Professor gazed out the window at the helicopters and media camps set up in the distance. "There are only two Gears left to find. It won't be long before we will have to leave—to go with Sam to find the Dream Gate. I fear if we wait till the very last moment to make our move, we will find it impossible to make the journey alone."

"So where will we go?" Zara asked, still looking nervous.

"Everyone in the world knows who we are," Rapha added.

"Don't worry, there is someplace safe," the Professor replied. "I know, after everything you have witnessed, especially in these last few days, it may seem as if we have no one left to trust. But we still have friends on our side. The most important thing, above all else, is that we must make sure the last 13 are prepared for when the time comes to assemble the Bakhu machine."

"Prepared?" Xavier asked.

"Yes," the Professor said. "I know that all of you must be there and ready, right at the end."

"Are you talking about the prophecy?" Xavier said. On the wall, next to where he stood by the windows, was a printout of the Dream Stele hieroglyphs. A translation was written underneath.

Dreaming of their destiny,
Minds entwined, thirteen will be.
Falter not, the last cannot fall,
Or Solaris shall rule over all.

One by one each shall unveil,
A Gear they need so to prevail.
Dream a path through time and space,
There to find the sacred place.

Something about it bugged him. But what? He remembered the night at the museum, when he'd seen Sam and Lora in police uniforms, before he knew about all this, how his father's sponsored exhibition of antiquities found by Dr. Kader had been attacked by Egyptian Guardians. He stared absently at the words.

"You mean the prophecy, saying that the last 13 will come together," Maria said.

"That's right," the Professor said, standing next to her and Xavier. "All of you—and the two we don't yet know the identity of—will be there at the end."

Xavier stared at the English translation words of the prophecy. Then the hieroglyphs.

"Xavier?"

"Professor—you said, 'I know that all of you must be there' . . ." He looked up to the old man. "What makes you so sure of that? It's more than just the prophecy, isn't it?"

"I dreamed it," the Professor said, chuckling. "You *are* your father's son, that's for sure—an inquisitive mind and a knack for reading people."

Yeah, and I can tell he's still holding something back.

"What is it?" Xavier asked him. "There's something else."

It took a while for the Professor to speak, and when he did, his voice was soft. "I fear, Xavier, that your journey will be harder than most."

"So do I," Xavier said, looking at the floor. "I've seen it in my dreams."

The others in the room were silent, their faces betraying their surprise and concern.

"I know," the Professor said.

"You do?" Xavier replied, recalling his week of nightmares that he'd not shared with anyone. "But you said we weren't recording dreams anymore, that it wasn't safe with all the prying eyes and ears focused on us now."

"True, but there are more ways that Dreamers can see," the Professor said, "and you don't get to be as ancient as me without getting a little wise."

"So, we're leaving for Egypt," Xavier said, certain now. He realized in that moment that he suddenly had great responsibility for what the group was about to do.

We're following my dreams.

The Professor nodded.

"To stay with my father—he's there now," Xavier said. "Has been for a few days."

"Is that safe?" Cody asked the Professor. "Won't people be expecting Xavier to be with his father?"

"No one knows he is there," Xavier said.

"Xavier is right," the Professor said. "His father has been preparing for us."

"Because of him—and because of Ahmed . . ." Xavier trailed off, then he understood. "That's why they've been working there in Egypt all these years and it's the reason behind all his work on the Dream Gate. That's why we have to go there, all of us."

"Yes," the Professor said, then turned to the others. "Dr. Dark is going to meet you in Egypt with representatives of the Enterprise."

"Is Egypt safe?" Zara asked.

"I heard there were riots there," Maria said.

"And that millions are having nightmares," Zara added.

"There is unrest everywhere," the Professor said, his voice tinged with concern. "But I promise you, every precaution will be taken to make sure you are all safe," he added.

"Where will you be?" Poh asked.

"I will join you," the Professor said, "but I have something else to attend to first."

ALEX

Alex stood before a smooth stone wall. It was the size of the side of a house and blocked off the natural cave.

Unlike the floor, this wall was not inscribed or carved at all. It was flat, straight and impossibly perfect, as though erected from a single slab of stone.

Definitely not natural, then.

And it was not that thick. Banging on it with a rock in his fist, it sounded as though it was a stone drum, and Alex could hear the reverberating echoes on the other side.

"Maybe it's not a wall at all . . ." His eyes traced the edges, where it met the floor and the ceiling. "Maybe it's a door."

You must be delirious now. A door—this big?

"A door with no handle," Alex said to himself after inspecting every corner and seam, "makes it a wall. A flat, thin wall, somehow brought here and placed in this cave . . . but why?"

He looked around the decorated chamber one last time.

So maybe it's an entrance to something—built a long, long time ago, when this land was habitable.

Alex chuckled. *Too impossible, surely?*

As Alex repacked his backpack, he remembered what he'd learned about Antarctica in geography class and from Ahmed—that it had once been part of a larger land mass and had broken off from Africa and Australia. But that was a long, long time ago.

"Maybe a boat was marooned down here once," Alex said, taking a final glance at the carvings. "Stuck, like me, and they made this place."

Dr. Kader would know.

Alex chucked his pack over his shoulders and pulled the straps tight, then zipped up his snowsuit and headed for where the daylight was creeping in the mouth of the cave.

"That . . . will . . . do it."

Alex sat down to test his handiwork. On the exposed side of the mountain he'd stacked some blocks of snow and ice against the wind. It needed more height, but he hunkered down, too tired to do more work now.

Alex pressed the emergency button on the GPS locator and hoped that it would work. He pulled out the thermos that he'd tucked between his suit layers, sipping the snow that had melted from his body warmth. Only a few drops fell into his dry mouth. He shook it over his mouth, hoping for a little more, but there was none—it was still packed with snow from the last time he'd stopped and refilled it.

The hike up the mountain had taken two hours and he'd drunk the last of his water in the ascent.

He pulled the tin cup from his pack, crammed it full of snow and placed it over a chemical fire cube sitting on the metal stand.

Alex looked around. He was on top of the first ridge of the mountainside that soared up next to the thermal valley, almost directly above the cavern he'd sheltered in. He could not see it for low-lying fog, but the sea was somewhere to the north, over the flat expanse of snow and ice. Behind him the mountains grew taller, rocky and craggy and frozen, impassable to an amateur with no climbing equipment.

He sat, tapped the GPS unit, and rattled it next to his ear.

"It'll work. Has to work. They'll find me."

It was cold and windy sitting there. He rebuilt the snow wall to be as high as his head, so the wind whipping along from the west wouldn't cut into him, making him even colder. He fashioned a domed roof from smaller packed bricks of snow. He ate his last cookie and checked what he had left. Two powdered soups, tea bags, a tube of sweetened milk, a small package of crackers and a tin of sardines.

Eurgh.

Alex didn't like sardines. He didn't like any creature that you had to eat whole, like mussels or oysters, or bugs and insects for that matter.

"But, if I'm still out here tomorrow," he said, checking his tin cup full of snow over the broken chemical block that was now glowing hot, "I'll eat them. Nibble the sides. *Maybe.*"

He checked the radio again. There was nothing but static. He looked up at the mountain behind him.

Maybe I should go higher, get better reception?

It'll have to be tomorrow . . . too tired . . . and it's too windy.

He checked the wall of his snow cave and hunkered down. He flexed his fingers and toes, then pulled the hood further down over his face. He already missed the warmth of the rock cave.

Whoever built that place was way smarter than me.

SAM

O utside, the Guardians and Jabari finished loading the Academy's new plane.

Technically, Sam thought, the aircraft wasn't *new*.

Nor was it, technically, the Academy's.

It was the aircraft that Sam had seen at Duke's farmhouse back in Texas when Tobias had acquired it from Stella.

Nice. Still, she'd taken it from the Enterprise, and what's left of the Enterprise have sided with us, so I suppose it does belong to us after all.

"You OK?" Lora asked Sam, noticing him lost in his thoughts.

"Yeah, fine," he said, pulling up his collar against the crisp morning air.

Cold? This ain't nothing—it's going to be freezing soon.

"Just thinking about this plane. About the last time I saw it . . . about Tobias."

"I know," Lora said. "He would want this, Sam, you know that. He'd want you to go on, to see this through and finish it. He'd have loved to have been out here right now with you."

"Yeah, I know," Sam said, smiling.

They watched the flight crew prepare the aircraft. The powerful motors hummed into life.

Jabari gave a thumbs-up that everything was ready for takeoff.

"You guys coming?" Eva asked them as she waited at the bottom of the aircraft's stairs, Arianna and Gabriella already aboard.

"C'mon, let's roll," Lora said, smiling and giving Sam a nudge towards the stairs.

"OK," Lora said, coming down the aisle to stand next to Sam. She produced a satellite phone. "I've got the Professor and Jedi on a secure communications link. We need to analyze your dream together and see what we can learn. We need to go over every detail so that we can stay ahead of the others."

Sam suddenly thought about what Lora was saying— *every detail*—and realized that, although he'd explained how there had been a "complication" with Alex, he hadn't fully described the scene he remembered from his dream. A wave of shame rippled over him.

It was only a dream. I can change things . . .

"OK," Sam said, taking a deep breath before speaking into the handset. "Hey, guys."

"Sam!" Jedi's excited voice came over the phone's loudspeaker. "Dude, I think we should probably start with what you did to Alex . . . tell me everything."

The plans for their Antarctic voyage had been decided and gone over, and everyone was ready. They seemed to take the situation with Alex in their stride, not judging Sam for what he did in his dream.

Sam looked out the window. The supersonic aircraft was getting them there in a hurry.

We'll be in Antarctica soon.

Sam thought he could make out drift ice and icebergs floating in the dark sea.

That's an amazing sight. I really have been all over the world now.

What an incredible ride.

I wonder where it will all end?

Lora came back from the cockpit and sat down in the empty seat beside Sam. "Another hour until we touch down. Remember, where we're landing, they don't know the real reason why we're there."

Sam could see her hesitate, as though there was something else she needed to share but was hanging on to it.

"Lora?" he asked.

She showed them her tablet.

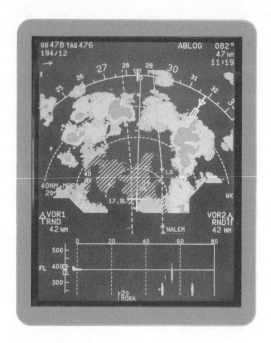

"The weather," Lora said. "It's going to get worse, and soon. We don't have much time on the ground to find Alex."

"How long?" Sam asked.

"Six hours, maybe a little more, at the most."

"And what will happen out there in six hours?" Eva asked.

"We can't be there," Lora said. "It's two polar vortexes converging to form a supercell. Half the continent will be in cyclonic blizzard conditions. Worst case, if we get caught out, we head for the closest station from Alex's last known location. Here." She tapped the map.

"The Chilean station?" Eva said. "OK."

"So," Sam said, "when we touch down, we have only six hours to find Alex *and* the Gear?"

Lora nodded. Eva looked ill at the thought of what was to come. The other two girls were sleeping. The Guardians and Agents were huddled at the end of the cabin, busy checking over their equipment and weapons.

Sam worried about Alex. If he had any locator device with him, he either hadn't activated it or it wasn't giving out enough of a signal.

Sam pulled out his phone, uselessly typing a text message to Alex. He looked at it for a long time before slowly hitting the delete button over and over, erasing the message.

Nope, it really is time for us to meet face-to-face.

"How far away do you think Alex is?" Eva asked.

Sam was silent, then he looked to her and Lora and saw that they expected him to know.

"Oh, me?" he said, looking at a map of Antarctica. "Well, ah, he's probably not far. I mean, I saw that mountain range in my dream, to the east. So near there?"

"OK," Lora said. "That's a pretty big search area. It could take days to cover."

"But we don't have days," Sam said, distractedly. "We'll find him. Unless he . . ."

"What?" Eva said to him. "Unless he what?"

"Sam?" Lora prompted.

Sam looked up and saw that his two friends were looking at him, eyes wide.

"Well?" Eva said.

"Unless . . . you see, my worry is," Sam began, pausing before carrying on, "well, how do you find a Dreamer if he doesn't want to be found—because he's not on our side anymore?"

XAVIER

Xavier frowned.

The Professor's not coming? Where would he have to be that was more important than this?

Xavier looked at his friends' faces, wondering how they would cope in Egypt, if—no, *when*—things got complicated.

"What if we're not ready?" Maria asked, apparently having the same thought.

"You will be," the Professor replied. "All of you. Every dream you've ever had has prepared you for what will be coming."

Xavier looked at the floor.

What if I'm not ready . . . ?

"You'll be ready too, Xavier," the Professor said. "Self-doubt is natural. Believe in yourself, in your part of the prophecy."

The students left in a tight group, talking quietly but animatedly, a spring and purpose in their step as they left to pack—but Xavier hung back.

"Professor . . ."

"Yes, Xavier?" The Professor looked up wearily from where he stood at his desk.

"I'm not sure about this," Xavier said, looking back down the hall and watching his friends depart. "I mean, I've had a dream—a dream I've had all week. It's always the same but each time I see more and more. And it was, well . . . it was dangerous."

"And in these dreams you were in Egypt?"

"That's right."

"I know," the Professor said. "It was the same in my dream too. But don't worry, you'll be fine."

"Have you seen the end—right up to the Dream Gate?" Xavier asked, hope in his voice at the prospect of knowing the future.

"No, I've only seen small glimpses, of us in Egypt, of the sun rising and setting. Of thirteen figures in the shadows, all coming together. After that, nothing."

"And you're staying here?" Xavier's eyes searched the Professor's for some sign of apprehension, but he saw none. It made Xavier feel better, seeing that the Professor's expression was certain.

"For the moment. This is how it is destined to be, Xavier," the Professor said. "Those here, those working with us, those working against us, we all have unique parts to play. Like gears in a machine, you might say."

"Even Solaris?" Xavier said. "He has a part to play?"

"Even Solaris. Think of it as yin and yang, light and dark, day and night."

"Like dreams and nightmares," Xavier said, "they're both always there?"

"That's right," the Professor said. "For Dreamers, nightmares are important too—they show us events that may happen and we can strive to prevent them, or at least prepare for them."

"So, they're a blessing *and* a curse."

"Exactly!" the Professor said, smiling. "And for the rest of the world, the seven billion souls around the globe that sleep every night, their nightmares show them that there are ways to do things, ways to change. Perhaps even ways to prepare."

"So it's the same for all of us."

"The whole world is connected by dreams. It is just that Dreamers are aware of it, at the front lines if you will, driving the dream wave for the rest."

"We learned that in class," Xavier said. "I remember learning about changing the endings of nightmares. How when we have recurring nightmares, we can change what happens—like, we can beat what's terrifying us."

"That's right. Have you tried it, with your own nightmares?"

"Yes," Xavier said. "I've come up with different endings. I've rehearsed them, awake and then just before I sleep, just like we were taught, to remind myself that I don't have to have that ending, preparing should the nightmare occur again."

"How has it worked for you?"

Xavier shook his head. "I've tried everything, but I can't change it."

The Professor paused. "This is the dream of your father dying?" he asked in a quiet voice.

Xavier nodded.

"There's still time, Xavier," the Professor said. "There's still time for another ending."

SAM

"**R**emember!" Lora said loudly, to be heard over the engines as their aircraft turned in the air for the landing approach. "No one down there knows our real purpose, so keep it to yourselves."

"It's just a 'rescue mission,'" Sam replied across the aisle with a thumbs-up. "Got it. And whatever we do, don't mention the Gear that forms part of a machine that will lead to the Dream Gate and help us save the world."

Gabriella laughed, Arianna was tight-lipped. Sam wondered if the Russian was pleased to be back among so much snow. Outside Sam's window, he saw what would be their base of operations: Crawley Station.

It was doughnut-shaped, with a central structure in the middle and two outer rings, connected by corridors at each point of the compass. From the air it looked small, but, as they neared, it grew to be a complex that could easily house fifty researchers. There were some outer buildings too, domes poking up into the air, a large one next to the icy runway.

Two figures were standing out in the cold, dressed in

bright-red snowsuits. They had orange burning flares in their hands, using them to direct the pilots. The jet touched down and they taxied to the largest of two cigar-shaped buildings, which looked like it served as an aircraft hangar. The engines died down as soon as the jet was inside.

"Wow," Sam said as he left the aircraft, walking down the fold-down stairs at the back of the jet between the undercarriage, pulling his Stealth Suit up around his face as he moved. Like the rest of his friends, he also had a yellow snowsuit over the top. But the wind still shocked the senses, blowing snow and ice through the air as it blasted through the huge hangar doors.

The aircraft's engines had wound down and four station crew emerged from the hangar and went about running a fuel line. Sam figured that in this environment, there was no way a vehicle could stay idle for long and still be expected to work. The large building was full of equipment. Through an open door, Sam could just make out a helicopter, wrapped up against the cold, and several large red snowcats—boxy reinforced vans with thick tank treads instead of tires.

Their jet would be taking off once it was refueled, returning to collect them the next day.

No way out until then. And a clock ticking to find Alex.

"And don't forget," Lora said as they shuffled behind Jabari and the others towards the door of the main base, "stay close at all times."

Ahead, a huge yellow door, the outer air lock, hissed open as they neared.

Sam checked his watch as they entered the base.

Just under six hours to go . . .

A greeting party had formed in the mess hall. All the station crew were dressed in the same red snowsuits. Twelve of them in total. A short man with red hair, a thick moustache and yellow-tinted glasses introduced himself as Dr. Roberts.

Lora introduced everyone as hot drinks were handed out while preparations got underway for their rescue mission.

"We're ready to go when you are," Dr. Roberts said finally, his voice deep but quiet.

"Thank you, we will be ready in five minutes," Lora said.

"Do you have any idea where your missing friend might be?" Dr. Roberts asked.

"We have his last known location," Lora said. "He's been stationary for some time."

"Hmm," Dr. Roberts said. "Does he have a tracking device?"

"Something like that," Lora said. She pointed at the big rugged cases that the Guardians were carrying. "Can we set up our communications gear here before we leave?"

"Of course," Dr. Roberts said, "follow me."

Lora followed, leaving Sam and the others with the rest of the Guardians and several of the crew.

"Well, that was weird," Eva said quietly, sipping a hot chocolate. "Dr. Roberts, I mean."

"Really?" Sam replied, adding extra sugar to his hot drink. "Was it the thick red moustache? Or the nasally voice?"

"What do you mean?" Gabriella said.

"Oh, I don't know," Eva said, adding marshmallows. "He just didn't seem very concerned."

"Maybe that's how they do things down here?" Sam said. "These scientists are used to living in pretty harsh conditions. I suppose that makes you tough, otherwise you wouldn't survive. And rescuing someone stuck out there is a big ask. Storm or not, in this environment, time's always ticking. And right now, we've got under six hours."

"Yeah, I guess . . ." Eva said as Lora came back into the mess hall with Dr. Roberts.

"OK, remember the plan," Lora said. "Eva, Gabriella and Arianna, you're staying here with Harry and Larry." She pointed to the two closest Guardians. "Stay in contact with Jedi via our communications and monitoring equipment. The rest of us will join Dr. Roberts and his crew who have volunteered to assist us crossing the ice to Alex's last known location. It's about an hour's drive from here in those big snowcats."

"OK," Sam said, looking meaningfully at Eva.

See, they're helping us out.

"Let's roll," he said.

"Good luck out there," Eva said. She leaned towards Sam and whispered, "But be quick. I don't like this place."

The wind blew up a wall of snow that whipped across the frozen ground. Sam watched as their driver ignored the view through the windshield, instead relying on the GPS and radar to navigate ahead.

And he's no slouch, even in these conditions.

The three snowcats rumbled across the ice like mini tanks in a race. Inside, the sound of the engine running at full speed was almost deafening. Dr. Roberts sat up front next to their driver, Sam seated behind him next to Jabari, with two of Dr. Roberts's station crew at the rear. Every now and then they'd hit a ridge of ice and the snowcat would become airborne and crash back to earth with a bone-shuddering thump.

"Just another day in the office?" Sam called out to Dr. Roberts, trying to make conversation in the harsh silence.

The flame-haired station chief remained silent as he cross-checked their bearings, tapped the GPS screen mounted on the dashboard and pointed out at the view of white beyond their glass windshield, indicating a slight adjustment to their heading.

"I guess so . . ." Sam said under his breath.

Ahead of them in another snowcat was Lora, their Guardians and Agents, and another three station crew. The huge box shape of the vehicle was a blur in the snow, a red smudge that they were chasing. Close behind them, another 'cat rumbled on with the station's medical team inside.

Hang on, Alex, we're coming . . . and I sure hope you're pleased to see us.

"You think this super storm could be hitting us earlier than we thought?" Sam asked Jabari. "I mean, this wind, it's crazy."

The Egyptian Guardian leader shook his head. "No," he said. "This is just the fringe of it, the weather that's being pushed out to make way for what's coming. Believe me, when it hits, you'll know it."

Sam gulped. He couldn't imagine worse weather than this. Jabari didn't appear concerned.

"You've been in a snowstorm like this before?" Sam asked.

"No," Jabari replied, his lean tanned face behind his dark beard showing no emotion. "Not snow. But sand, yes. I have been in sandstorms that have lasted for days and engulfed entire towns. Buried them, as though they never existed."

"I think I'd prefer that," Sam said. "Least it wouldn't be cold."

Jabari shrugged. "The desert is cold at night. And the sand that blows with the storm winds? It gets everywhere. *Everywhere*. And when it never seems to end, it's frightening."

"Great," Sam said. "OK, then I think I'll stick to the tropics. An island maybe." He watched the GPS monitor and looked at the radar screen showing the three dots of their convoy as they moved towards the blinking green dot.

Alex.

10

XAVIER

"Think we will ever be back at the Academy again?" Maria asked.

"Sure," Xavier said, trying to sound relaxed and upbeat. "Definitely. Just a short detour first to the safest place in the world."

"Nowhere is completely safe," Phoebe said, driving their van. "Even where we are going. You have to remember that. You need to stay alert, OK?"

Xavier nodded. The others did too. They all knew it. Too much had happened to think otherwise. As they drove on in the darkness, undetected by the UN guards or the waiting media throngs, he could tell that Phoebe was frustrated about not being able to go to Antarctica.

Phoebe probably had to come with us instead of going after Alex because they're worried she might be too emotionally attached.

He couldn't blame her for being anxious. Xavier, along with the others, had been told about the huge storm that was sweeping across Antarctica—time really was against them all.

"Yeah," Cody said from his seat next to Xavier. "I'd believe that. The stuff I've seen. Solaris—" he trailed off as if reliving it.

Xavier looked to where his fellow last 13 Dreamers sat. He was the only one of them still with his Stealth Suit switched to match its surrounds, blending in to appear invisible, the feature they'd used to slip past the security cordon around the Academy.

Not that we were prisoners there, Xavier reminded himself.

The need to be secretive about their departure was crucial. If it became known that the last 13 were on the move, the world would want to move with them.

We've got the world behind us but we can't risk using any of their armies in case they decide to take over the race, or the Gate, for themselves. Then what use to us are they?

The director had warned them that there wasn't a country in the world that didn't want the prophesied "ultimate power" beyond the Dream Gate.

Trust no one, he'd said.

"Solaris' Suit can't be better than these Stealth Suits, can it?" Cody said, bringing Xavier back to the present. He changed his Suit several times, until he settled on an outfit. "I mean, he never changes *his* appearance like we do. Maybe he doesn't have the ability to blend into his environment and be invisible."

"Are you sure?" Maria said. "Maybe he can."

"And he just doesn't need to," Poh added.

Cody paused, thinking about it, then shrugged.

"Truth is," Xavier said, looking to his friends, "we don't know much about Solaris at all, do we? I mean, who's behind that mask? It could be anyone."

"And who knows what he can do?" Rapha said. "Who knows what he's really capable of?"

The others fell silent. Phoebe drove on, the headlights piercing the dark of the empty road to London.

"I think that *is* the one thing we do know about him," Xavier said, his voice firm. "Solaris is capable of anything and everything."

"And that's all we need to know," Phoebe added.

"What's the matter, Cody?" Xavier said, the last to board the plane. "You never been on a private jet before?"

Cody looked around in awe. "I've been in plenty of small, private aircraft," he replied, sitting in one of the plush leather chairs. "Just nothing this . . . fancy."

"Is this really your father's?" Poh asked, looking uneasy in the luxurious surroundings.

"Yeah," Xavier replied, sitting opposite Phoebe and feeling self-conscious. He liked the perks that came with having a successful businessman for a father, but he wanted to fit in with the others too. He shrugged. "It's a family business."

"Must be some business," Cody said, nervously fiddling with his entertainment screen.

"The business of dreams," Phoebe said, "can be quite profitable."

"Sure looks like it," Cody said. "Beats running a little tour company in Arizona like my family did."

"Well, that's not all they did, though, is it?" Xavier said, one eyebrow raised.

"So, your dad will be waiting for us in Egypt?" Maria asked, changing the subject.

"Ah, yeah, that's what the Professor said," Xavier said, buckling in. "We'll be there before you know it."

"What is he like?" Rapha asked.

"My dad?" Xavier said. Rapha nodded. "Well . . . he's—I guess he's pretty awesome. Works hard, away from home a lot, doing his psychiatrist dream work around the world wherever Dreamers need him the most. Running our family company, does all kinds of stuff. Funding expeditions to find Dreamer stuff from history. He's . . . he's always been busy. As long as I can remember."

"Did you always know you were a Dreamer?" Rapha asked.

Xavier shook his head. "No, my dad never let on. Sent me to a 'normal' school too, instead of the Academy. That's where I met Sam."

"I always knew I was a Dreamer," Cody said, looking more relaxed now. "I wonder why your dad never told you about the world of Dreamers."

"I guess he wanted me to work it out myself, in my own time," Xavier said.

"Gotta make you wonder, though," Cody said, closing his eyes and tilting his chair back, "what else has he kept from you?"

"Xavier?" Phoebe woke him. He'd been dreaming, the same dream about his father again. Though this time, he was somewhere deep and dark that suddenly became bright when he woke. "We're nearly there."

He sat up and looked around. The others were asleep. He checked his watch—five in the morning, London time.

"Did you sleep?" he asked Phoebe.

"No," she replied, "but don't worry about me. It's you and the others that need rest."

"You're worried about Alex," Xavier said, "in Antarctica."

Phoebe nodded. "Yes."

"Any word?" Xavier said. "Any trace of him?"

Phoebe shook her head. "We have some information, but it's not enough. Jedi's looking, Shiva too. A few search and rescue crews from bases down there have been out. But the storm is getting closer."

"Sorry." Xavier could see that Phoebe was tired and pale from being so stressed. "Phoebe, Alex will be OK.

He's there, at the end. I know it."

"You dreamed it?"

"Yes," Xavier replied. "The Professor too. We are all there at the Gate."

Phoebe nodded and said, "Thank you, Xavier. And I want to believe that. But you know dreams can change—as things change in real life, so they change in dreams."

"Not this one," Xavier said. "He'll be there. You'll see."

Phoebe allowed herself a small smile. "And the thirteenth Dreamer? Have you seen who that is?"

"No . . . but then that's not *my* job," Xavier said, and Phoebe laughed.

11

ALEX

It was the movement that woke Alex. At first he'd thought it was a dream, a dream where he was flying high above the snow, close enough to the sun so that he was warm. But it wasn't warm. It was cold. He was hungry. He was alone.

But then he heard a voice. "Alex . . ."

Alex felt as though he were floating between the dream world and the waking one, not all awake yet, not asleep either. It was cold. He concentrated on keeping warm.

"I've found him! Over here!"

Dr. Kader?

"Alex!"

Alex opened his eyes. Blinding white light crashed in.

"Am I . . . ?"

"Alex!" Ahmed said again.

Alex squinted against the sun to see Dr. Kader pulling him from his snow cave.

"Am I . . . dreaming?" Alex asked as he looked around.

"No, no. This is quite real," Ahmed said, smiling.

Relief flooded through him, almost making him pass out.

Not dying in a snow cave. Not today.

But how——?

"You . . . Hans . . . the rope . . ." Alex said. "I'm so sorry."

"Don't worry about that now," Ahmed said. "And it's quite all right. I'm certain I would have cut the ropes too in your position, ha! And we are all OK. Now, are you able to stand?"

"Yeah, I think so," Alex said, slowly getting up and working the cold stiffness from his legs. Looking back inside his makeshift sleeping hole, he saw his backpack, which he'd used as a pillow, and the radio, still with its tall antenna poking up. "You traced the signal?"

Ahmed shook his head.

"Then how'd you find me?" Alex asked.

"Well," Ahmed said, "remember those shots in the arm we all had on the way down here, the vitamin boosters?"

"Yeah . . ." Alex had a vague recollection of the medical they'd had on board the *Ra*.

That's right, we did get shots! Huh, my brain has turned to mush out in the cold. Geez.

"Turns out they included some kind of tracking device."

"But why?" Alex subconsciously rubbed his arm where he'd taken the shot.

"For just this kind of situation, I would think."

"Who were you calling out to before?" Alex asked.

"Over the other side, come look," Ahmed said. He helped Alex shake out the numbness from his body and walked higher up the mountain. He motioned to the lip of a high stone ledge. Alex clambered up and looked down to the icy plain below. He squinted against the brightness of the day on the white surface, his hand raised against the fierce sunshine cutting through the clear sky.

A team was spread out on the snow plain below. Hans, unmistakable in his bright-yellow snowsuit, stood near a heavy-lift aircraft on the ice—and a lot of guys in snowsuits, who'd been scouring the mountain looking for Alex and were now moving down to the aircraft.

"I found something, near a thermal spring," Alex said, hoisting his backpack over his shoulder and following Dr. Kader down the mountain.

"So did we, Alex," Ahmed replied. "So did we."

As they approached Hans, Alex stopped at a hole that had been cut into the ice. How they'd cut it he was unsure, but it must have involved huge saws or something. It was about the size of a bus.

"Similar stuff to thermite," Ahmed said. "Burns hot and fast, right down through the ice."

Hans walked over to them, smiling broadly. "Alex!" he bellowed. "How marvelous to have found you once again. That was a lucky escape for all of us, eh? What an adventure!"

Lucky for me they don't seem to be holding a grudge.

"It's good to see you too," Alex replied. "But how did you—I mean . . ."

"How are we not all dead?" Hans said, laughing at Alex's horrified face. "Lady Luck was on our side, my friend. After an exciting but horrifying slide down a very large crevasse, we landed in relative safety in a lower snow field. Our guide sustained a minor injury, but he'll live."

"Hans found some higher ground and radioed for assistance," Ahmed added.

"I like to think of that as my hero hour," Hans said, Ahmed rolling his eyes behind him. "But come, come, follow me," Hans said, heading towards a ladder hooked over the hole in the ice. In the water ten feet below was the submersible.

Alex followed Hans and Dr. Kader down the ladder. With every rung he descended, Alex felt an ever-increasing weight sink into his stomach. Whether it was fear about what unknown dangers lay ahead, or if it was his dream of Sam, he was unsure. What he did know, what he was *certain* of, was that today would not end well.

"Position marked," the sub pilot called out.

"Position confirmed, continue," the copilot replied.

Alex stared at the screen showing their progress

through the ice. The sub's powerful lights lit up the underside of the ice sheet, the world before them shining every shade of cold blue.

"Position marked," the pilot said.

"Confirmed. Continue."

They went on like that for ten minutes, plotting out their course slowly, following a route that they'd apparently taken a few hours before.

"It was incredible," Hans said to Alex, seated facing him across the sub's cargo area. "My team followed the overland route plotted in my grandfather's log book and took measurements of the ice below. I believe it is navigable the whole way, under the ice, to the point marked."

"So you've been under the ice?"

"No—not yet," Hans replied. "We cut through the ice with thermite to meet up with the sub."

Alex nodded, looking at the screen once more. The thought of untold tons of ice overhead sent a shiver through him.

It's OK—I'll be OK. I mean, I would have seen it, if I was crushed like an empty soda can, right? In my dream? Surely.

Surely . . .

"It's OK, Alex," Hans said. "We'll be there in—"

"Contact," the pilot called. "Dead ahead."

All eyes moved to the monitors. Up ahead, another light emerged from the shadowy underwater world.

"Undersea rover in sight," the copilot announced. "One

hundred fifty feet. Continue on."

Alex watched as a little underwater robot came into view.

"It scouted the way," Hans said to Alex, not taking his eyes off the screen. "That's how we knew we had the right place . . ."

"What did it find?" Alex asked.

Hans was quiet for a while, and then he broke into a huge grin and pointed at the screen. "That!"

Alex looked at the monitor and nearly choked in shock.

12

SAM

Sam paused in his climb and caught his breath. He looked back. At the base of the mountain, the snowcats were parked close together to make a sheltered space between them. The wind was strong but the mountain blocked the worst of it. The sky was clear.

So far.

He looked up the mountain slope.

Lora was ahead of him, a GPS unit in her hand as she trekked to Alex's last known location. Dr. Roberts was close behind her, with Jabari and a couple of Guardians. They'd all stopped and were looking at the ground.

Sam ran to catch up. They stood in a little semicircle, pointing at the ground and looking around. He pushed through to see what they were crowded around, the nerves in his stomach clenching at the thought of what he might see . . .

Nothing. Nothing but snow.

"What is it?" Sam asked. "What's the big deal?"

"A sign," Lora said, crouching down.

"We're too late," Jabari replied, pointing.

Sam could then see what they were looking at—a little snow cave. It was easy to miss, just a small hollow in the snow. But it was man-made.

"You think Alex did that?" Sam asked.

"He must have slept in there," Lora said. She pointed, "Look!"

"What?" Sam said, seeing nothing but some little holes in the ground, as though someone had poked their finger into the snow at random intervals.

"It's a constellation," Lora said. "See?"

"Ophiuchus," Jabari said, crouched down. "The thirteenth constellation."

"Alex must have left it here as a sign, a marker," Lora said.

Sam looked around, as though hoping to see Alex not too far away, wandering the mountain, ready to be rescued. But there was nothing but the white of endless snow and the contrasting gray of rocky mountain outcrops.

Jabari walked off to the north, watching the ground like a hawk.

"But . . ." Sam's voice trailed off. "Where is he now?"

"I'm not sure . . ." Lora said, powering up the satellite phone to talk to Eva back at Crawley Station. Sam could hear her asking to relay the updated information to Jedi, who was doing everything he could to track Alex's location. Sam could imagine that perhaps somewhere high overhead an imaging satellite was scouring the frozen continent, looking through powerful cameras for Alex.

Be like looking for a needle in a haystack or for a dot on the sun. Or a drop in the ocean.

No. A speck in the snow—a single snowflake, somewhere on this icy, snow-covered continent.

Sam looked down the slope to the three snowcats parked at the foot of the mountain range. The Guardians and station crew were fanned out, looking for any footprints that might show where Alex had gone. But Sam knew they wouldn't have any luck. It was too flat and exposed down there—the wind would have covered any tracks by now. Even their own prints from just minutes ago were already virtually wiped out.

"Sam . . ."

He turned to see Jabari crouched away from the group.

"What is it?" Sam asked.

Jabari squatted close to the ground. "Footprints," he said.

"Really?" Sam looked hard and perhaps, at a certain angle, he could just make out the shape of the dents in the frozen snow. But they didn't really seem any different from the ground around them, the snow and ice blown and blasted by the weather. "You're sure they're footprints? Looks like, well, snow to me."

"Yes, I'm sure," Jabari said. "And someone else was with him—someone came across from the other side of the mountain and found him. Someone heavier, but with smaller feet. See?"

Jabari carefully scooped out soft snow from the compacted-snow prints, revealing them with more clarity.

"So there is!" Sam could see it more clearly now. There were two sets of prints, the shoes close to the same size but one set was double the depth.

Hans? Is Alex captive—or is he working with him? Has my friend gotten too close to them these past weeks and become brainwashed by Hans' goal of seizing the Dream Gate for himself?

"Can you track them?" Lora asked Jabari.

Jabari stood tall and nodded to her.

"Do it," Lora said. "Check in on the radio every twenty minutes. We'll take the snowcats and get around this mountain on the south side, since the tracks lead that way. Keep in touch and we will meet up on the other side."

"You've had a sighting of something?" Sam asked, seeing Lora's expression. "Something to the north?"

"Jedi has managed to detect Hans' boat moored there, a couple of miles out to sea," Lora said. "And from what he can see on deck, they must have lowered a submarine into the water."

"So what—they've gone *under* the ice sheet?" Sam said, looking out at the flat expanse of white. From up here, he could just make out the blue on the horizon that was the sea. "But then why would Alex trek up here, on the mountain? And alone?"

"Maybe they got separated," Jabari said, readying to leave.

Sam checked his watch, which showed a countdown on a small dial.

Just under five hours until the storm hits.

And still not much closer to finding Alex. But he was here. With someone else.

And Hans is close by with a sub.

"Can you really track them on foot?" Sam asked. The tracks seemed, by the direction that they were pointing, to head over the mountain pass and then down towards the seaward side to the north.

But then where? Back to the coast? To the submarine somehow?

Jabari tightened the straps on his pack. "I will try," he said. "You stay with Lora," he said to Sam. "See if you can get the vehicles around the other side of this mountain."

"I can help you," Sam said, eager to trek with the Guardian despite the cold and wind that he knew would blast him as soon as they crested the ridge of the mountain.

"No," Jabari said, setting off, watching the ground as he tracked. He called over his shoulder, "I work faster alone!"

EVA

"**S**o maybe Alex is with Hans again," Jedi said. "But if that keeps him safe, maybe that's a good thing."

"Urgh, Hans," Eva said, rolling her eyes. "Are we ever going to be rid of him? Actually, I wonder if—hang on a sec." She turned at the sound of the door handle turning.

Briony came in. Now that Dr. Roberts was gone with Sam and Lora and most of the crew, the head of the station was a woman named Briony. She was never far away from Eva, buzzing around and offering to help, coming into the lab every fifteen minutes or so to check in.

"You OK in here?" she asked.

"Yep," Eva answered. "Just like before. Still OK."

"You're sure?"

"Yep. Just like before, thanks."

"You don't need me to help out at all?" Briony asked, all smiles. "I know my way around communications equipment."

"Nope. All good, under control."

"Right, then."

"Great, thanks again."

Briony hovered by the door. "Well," she added, "just come over to the habitat if you need anything—you know where I am."

Eva smiled. "Will do."

Briony left, looking a little deflated.

"Wow," Jedi said over the video feed from the Enterprise's headquarters in Amsterdam. "She's a little too anxious to help out, yeah?"

"Ah, catching on to the weird Antarctic base vibe much?" Eva said, a shiver running through her. "Seriously, it's odd around here. That woman is in charge of the station now. She's been in and out of here constantly since the others left. I can't decide if she's trying to see what I'm up to and if there's any news, or if she's just that desperate for company."

"She's probably never been in charge before," Jedi said. "But remember, a lot of people know who you all are now. This race to save the world stuff affects people in different ways. If you think she's acting oddly, I'd stay alert—stay frosty!"

"Will do," Eva said. She looked to the empty doorway where Briony had stood. "She is definitely getting a bit annoying."

"These people have been in the cold too long," Jedi laughed. "You'll pull through. And what have you done with the others anyway? Where are Arianna and Gabriella?"

"Scouting around the base, checking everything out. They should be back soon."

"Well, you should have the live feed from our eye in the sky any . . . second . . . now. Almost now. One sec. Shoot, gotta change cables . . ."

Eva checked her watch, then frowned. "Sorry—live feed, you were saying?"

"What is it?" Jedi asked, seeing her concern.

"Now that I think about it," Eva said, looking to the door, "the others really should have been back by now."

It feels like something's not right—we agreed not to be apart too long, to stay safe.

We agreed on the time they'd return.

"I'm going to go and check on them," Eva said.

"But the satellite feed is coming through any moment," Jedi said. "You need to be here to handle the local radio calls to the search teams."

"I won't be long," Eva said, getting up.

"Eva, they're probably just not aware of the time. You have a job to do now, keeping Lora in the loop."

"You're right, they're probably just messing around," Eva said. "But I have to be sure, Jedi. We promised each other. You keep an eye on things here for me, I'll be back in a flash of the aurora australis."

Eva left the room, leaving Jedi at the other end of the line facing an empty chair.

Eva walked through the tech wing towards the accommodation pods. There was no one in sight.

Where is everyone?

She stopped, just short of a half-open doorway ahead. The sign next to the door said TECH ROOM 2B.

The voices coming from within were not her friends'. But Eva stayed and listened. She could make out Briony's voice, as well as that of a tattooed guy she'd met earlier. And at least two other men's voices.

So there's four of them.

But what are they talking about?

She leaned closer to the door to hear better. Then she *did* hear what they were talking about.

They were talking about *her*.

"We should put a person in there with Eva," Briony said.

"I can go Stealth and hide in there," another voice said. "She'll never know I'm there."

"That's good," Briony said. "Next time she's out of the room, sneak in. She can probably spot Stealth Suits in motion, so be wary."

"She won't leave the room," the tattooed man said. "She's smart. They'll work in shifts, her and her friends, so that there's always someone in there to talk to the others out in the snow."

"That won't be a problem," Briony said, and even from outside the door, Eva could detect the smile in her voice. "I've already taken care of her friends."

Before Eva could react, she heard footsteps behind her.

14

"**W**hy are we stopping?" Sam asked.

Dr. Roberts didn't answer. Instead, he simply got up from his seat and went to the back of the snowcat's cargo area where he started talking quietly to the rest of his crew.

Sam turned to look questioningly at Lora, who was now traveling in his snowcat.

"Must be too dangerous to go on," Lora guessed, looking out the windshield at the frozen ground that spread before the mountain and headed to the sea. "Even though they have GPS, if you can't see where you're going out here, you could find yourself driving into a crevasse. And if the ice thins out, we could get stuck, or worse. These beasts are heavy."

"Fair enough. We don't really want either of those things to happen," Sam said, looking back as one of the crew exited the vehicle and trudged over to one of the other vehicles, no doubt to relay messages about how to progress.

"Probably not."

Sam checked his watch.

Four hours until the super storm hits.

Find Alex and the Gear before then.

No pressure.

"How long do we give Jabari out there on his own?" Sam asked Lora.

"Not long," Lora said, tapping her satellite phone, trying to get a better signal. "Not today."

"What else can we do?" Sam asked.

"Not much . . ." Lora was preoccupied with the phone.

Sam looked out the window at the wind that whipped up snow, spraying it against the windows, and a shiver ran through him.

Least it's warm in this tin can with the engine running and the heaters blazing.

Outside, he could just make out the other two snowcats that had stopped alongside them, the big red machines stopped in the snowdrift that the wind kicked up, the mountains no longer shielding them from the increasingly wild weather.

"Hey, has Jabari checked in yet?" Sam asked.

Lora was still looking at her phone, twisting dials and pushing buttons.

"Lora? It's past the check-in time."

"No word from him yet, but now the phone's not working at all. Must be this vehicle interfering with the satellite signal, or maybe it's the storm front," Lora said.

"I'll go outside and see if I can get it to work."

Lora left her seat and headed into the cargo bay, where all their massive snowsuits were hanging up.

Sam drummed his fingers on his knees, tapping out a tune to a song he'd not heard in ages. He fumbled around for his phone in his Stealth Suit pocket. No signal.

Man . . . how long are we going to be stuck here?

"It's going to be a while before a signal gets through," Lora said, rejoining Sam. "They said that the weather radar is showing this front blasting us for about an hour, and then there should be some calmer conditions. The front preceding the storm has electrical activity. We might even be able to see it."

"The aurora australis?" Sam said. "I saw the northern lights, the aurora borealis, in Canada once, it'd be amazing to see the southern ones too."

"I've never seen either," Lora said. "Do they really look like bands of brilliant green lights shimmering through the sky?"

"Yep, it's quite amazing," Sam said.

"Hmm, all that energy, power, visible to the eye," Lora said. "Charged particles colliding in the atmosphere. Something to do with the solar winds and Earth's magnetic field lines? Tobias would know more—he'd certainly have explained it better."

"He'd explain it and it'd take him hours." Sam smiled ruefully. "Plus we'd have to put up with his lame science jokes along the way."

Lora gave him a small smile. "I'll go and tell the others, give them an update on the storm. Hang tight—back in a flash."

"Yeah," Sam said, looking out his window. "Don't think I'll be going anywhere."

Sam sat and waited, drumming his fingers, hearing another of the Crawley crew getting into their heavy snowsuit as Lora opened the rear cargo ramp door and a rush of cold rolled in like a wave. The hiss of the door opening on the hydraulics was drowned out by the wind. Sam shuddered against it, the cold trickling down his spine, ice crystals turning to water as they hit his warm face and hands.

How you doing out here, Alex?

Sam looked out his window, his arms wrapped around himself as he waited for the door to hiss shut.

Will you still be my friend, when we meet?

Sam's thoughts were interrupted by Dr. Roberts, who sat down next to Sam with a heavy thump. Sam shifted a little to his left so as to not be rubbing shoulders with the guy. His breath stank like sweet coffee.

"Bad weather, huh?" Sam said, shifting over a little more.

Dr. Roberts remained silent.

"So, how much longer do you think we'll wait here?"

Silence.

"Bad storm coming, I hear."

Still nothing.

"Right, good chatting with you." Sam got up from his seat and looked out the front windows of the snowcat. He could just make out the silhouettes of Lora and another crew member nearing the next vehicle. There was nothing else to see but a world of white. He watched as they rapped on the outside of the cargo door to let them in.

Sam felt the presence of Dr. Roberts standing next to him, watching out the window too. Sam turned to look at him.

Odd moustache.

Sam looked back out the windows, seeing the cargo ramp of the neighboring snowcat starting to lower. But then he did a double take and felt the air sucking out of his lungs.

No sooner had the cargo ramp come down than the Crawley base crew member, standing just behind Lora, put something to Lora's neck. Sam watched in horror as his friend fell to the ground like a puppet with its strings cut.

15

ALEX

Alex had seen many unbelievable things in these last few months. This was one of them.

No. This takes the cake.

"This is . . ." Alex said.

"Incredible, isn't it?" Ahmed said.

"But . . ." Alex did not know what to say.

I am standing in an undersea world . . . like something from a movie.

Ferns gently waved all around him. *Ferns*—like, green, leafy, tropical rain forest type ferns.

In Antarctica!

He looked back to where the submarine had surfaced inside the underground cave. On the rocky shore, near where the mini-sub was moored, was an old, rusted submarine. It was huge, with torpedo tubes—just like the one he'd seen on the bottom of the ocean.

"The geothermal spring provides the heat, creating the steamy atmosphere," Hans called out. "Is it not amazing?"

"What about the light?" Alex said, looking up at the far-off ceiling that glowed in patches.

"It's ice," Ahmed explained, "ten feet thick in some places. It melts under this side—that's all the dripping you can hear hitting the pools—and is replenished above. I can't even imagine how long this ecosystem has been here."

Alex nodded. On all sides, the rocky ground was cracked and steam hissed from within.

"This is no ordinary mountain range," Hans said, leading the way. "We're inside an old volcano system. It's dormant, but there's still enough lava near the surface to create heat."

Alex followed them across the moss-covered ground, the sub pilots staying behind while two of Hans' guys led the way to the far end of the vast network of caves.

"This is what my grandfather rediscovered so many years ago," Hans said as they walked along.

"*Re*discovered?" Alex said to Hans. Ahmed was behind them, taking photographs. Alex picked a small pink flower that grew from the bottom of a stone wall and had a close-up look at a tiny lava tube opening next to it. It looked like a perfectly round, miniature tunnel.

Hans checked his notes, made from what he could piece together from his grandfather's journal, and motioned them forward towards another tunnel ahead. "He found the documents during the war," he replied, following his two men who lit the way ahead with powerful flashlights, "at the Dreamer Council's base under the Eiffel Tower."

"You mean he *stole* them from the Dreamer Council?" Alex said. The tunnel itself was another lava tube, similar to that which they'd navigated through underwater, but much smaller—this was maybe big enough to drive a van through.

"It was wartime," Hans replied, "sometime in 1940, I believe. Paris had fallen. It would be a few years before it would be liberated again. If not my grandfather, someone else would have taken the Dreamer Council's information, sooner or later." Hans looked to Alex and sighed. "Look," he went on, breathing heavily in the humid air, "he was in charge of antiquities during the war. He made sure they were safe. He protected the Dreamer Council's information, as well as items from many museums, galleries and private collections."

"And he found something mentioning this place?"

"Yes. It had been kept secret by the Council through the ages."

"And when he says 'through the ages,'" Ahmed said, walking next to Alex, "he means it. There have been rumors of this secret but nothing more. This place . . . we are going to be the first people to set foot here in over seventy years. And before then? Well, it may have been thousands of years since anyone else was here."

"Why'd he come here?" Alex asked. "Your grandfather?"

Hans smiled. "To hide things."

"It's getting hotter," Alex said, taking off another layer of clothing. He was now wearing just his shorts, T-shirt and boots. He packed his sweater into his backpack, along with his rolled-up snowsuit. Jogging to catch up to the others, he found Hans standing on a platform where the lava tube opened up into a dark cavern of black rock.

"The molten lava is nearer the surface here," Hans said, squeezing the sweat out of his hat. "We're close."

"Close to what?"

"Why don't you take a look and tell me?" Hans said.

Alex saw that Hans was motioning to where Ahmed and the others stood, hard to make out in the clouds of steam that rose from the ground. He walked cautiously over to them, keeping a sharp eye on the rocky ground beneath his feet. His flashlight was of little help in this place—it just got eaten up in the vastness. As he neared them, the steam cleared.

And he saw it.

Not another carved wall. Nothing to do with submarines or the last world war either.

It's a building.

It was an immense building, built into the volcano's conduit, where eons ago the massive mountain had erupted and spilled hot molten rock from the earth.

It was a building like some he'd seen before, in movies

and books and documentaries, never in real life. Not yet. But those buildings were on a different continent, far, far from here, and made of a different stone.

But there was no mistaking it.

It's a pyramid.

16

SAM

"What the . . ." Sam stopped dead when he felt the cool metal of a gun barrel press against his neck.

Oh no . . .

He turned to face the gunman, Dr. Roberts. At least, the short guy with the moustache and glasses with the name tag "Dr. Roberts" on his lapel.

"So, I'm guessing you're *not* Dr. Roberts," Sam said, his eyes going from the guy to the dart gun leveled at him, "head of the Crawley base?"

In reply, the guy took off his yellow-tinted glasses, then peeled off a fake nose and bushy moustache. Sam knew the guy behind the disguise.

Or rather, the woman.

Stella.

"If you move, Sam," she said, "I *will* hurt you."

The snowcats were up and running again. They were heading northeast this time, around the base of the mountains, skirting the glaciers, over the immense ice shelf that went out to sea some hundred miles away.

They don't seem concerned about the storm. Maybe they don't know about it?

So it wasn't that it was getting too dangerous to drive. They were plotting what to do with us, since Jabari left and there was a clear sign that Alex had been there. And Hans.

Well, now they've taken care of Lora. And the Guardians and Agents in the other snowcat are no doubt knocked out too.

That just leaves me . . .

Stella and her crew of rogue Agents maneuvered through the storm. They went slowly, in single file. Sam's snowcat was the middle vehicle, while Lora was unconscious, *or worse*, in the 'cat behind. Sam could barely bring himself to think about it.

The early bird may get the worm, Sam remembered Tobias telling him once, *but the second mouse gets the cheese.*

"If the lead vehicle falls in a crevasse, so be it?" Sam said to Stella, who sat opposite him eyeing a GPS screen.

"They know their mission," she replied without looking at him, watching the satellite readout of their movements via a blinking dot on the digital map. Sam could see two locations were labeled—one the last known location of Hans, the other the last sighting of Alex.

"There's a storm coming in, from the sea," Sam said. "Do you know that?"

Stella didn't reply.

"A real bad one," Sam said. "It'll blow these snowcats right off the ice shelf and into the water. Is that what you want?"

Stella still ignored him.

Great. But I have to figure a way out of this—a way to rescue my friends, to get to Alex, to get the Gear before all the others.

Need to stall for time.

"*Did* you try to kill me?" Sam asked. "That first time I was with Alex and Eva, on the helicopter. Did you shoot us out of the sky with missiles?"

"That wasn't me." Stella answered without looking at him. "We never fired at the helicopter. Those were my guys on board—they would have brought you, and Alex and Eva, directly to me that day. All this? It would have been very, very different."

So it really was the Egyptian Guardians.

"Why would I kill you, Sam?" Stella asked, looking at him. "Think about that. If you're dead—all this stops. You are the only person in the world who can see things that the others can't—you alone can understand all this, link the rest of the last 13 together."

"I think you're lying," Sam said. "You've been shooting at me and trying to blow me up the whole time!"

"Well, I *did* try to do without you, Sam," Stella sighed. "If I could have gotten that Tesla technology to work properly, I wouldn't need to be here now listening to you." She smiled. "Believe me, we're not that bad at what we do. If we'd wanted you dead, then that's how you'd be. *Dead*. But you're not. You're here. I haven't even darted you."

Right . . . so what does this mean? She needs me alive. That's good. But maybe she needs me conscious, right now, to lead her to Alex. How do I use that information? Could I rush her? Disarm her?

"Maybe you don't know everything," she went on. "Maybe, like your friend Alex who has been working with Hans, you have been working with the wrong group all along."

"What, working with you would have been better?" Sam said. "No thanks."

"Oh, poor us," Stella said. "Having you here as a hostage keeps us safe—you're our life insurance and our bargaining chip, should something go wrong. But it won't. Like I said, we're good at what we do."

"You're sure about all that?" Sam said. "You don't seem to have that many of the Gears for your boss, do you?"

Stella was silent, watching the screen that she held in her hands.

"And now you want Alex?" Sam asked. "And what about the next Dreamer? There's only one more Dreamer after him." He had to grab hold of his seat to stay steady as the snowcat roared full-speed over the uneven terrain of the ice shelf. "What then? You going to try getting all the Gears? The Academy will never give them to you."

"No." Stella leveled her cold gaze at him.

"No?" Sam said, challenging her. "Do you even know what you're doing? Because it doesn't seem like it."

"Do I want the machine? Sure." Stella smiled, and it was almost worse than her cold gaze. "I'm going to do what everyone else is going to do, Sam. Take the easiest option there is. Whoever has the machine, I will take it from them. Kill them, if we have to, why not? Then I'm going to go to Bakhu and switch the machine on. Then I will go to the Dream Gate. And, well, you know the rest."

Go to Bakhu? She talks about it like it's a place, not a machine.

Does she really know stuff about this that I don't?

"You really haven't got a clue. Playing at being the hero, saving the world, and you don't even understand the game. It's *pathetic*."

Sam's face burned and he looked away, gritting his teeth.

"Pity." Stella tapped the driver on the shoulder and pointed at her screen, signaling that they had to adjust their direction, before turning to Sam again. "You'll die ignorant, like the others. After we find the next Dreamer. You're the key, Sam, but only for these Gears and the machine. And after we unlock this, once we're at the Dream Gate, well then, what use is a key to something that we've already unlocked?"

Sam thought of the key hanging around his neck. He

thought about when he'd first seen it, on top of the Great Pyramid of Giza, when it had broken free from inside the crystal sphere, the Star of Egypt. The first Gear—*his* Gear.

"Not that thing hanging around your neck," Stella said, as though reading his mind. "*You*."

"You're so crazy for power, it's the very thing that will make it slip through your grasp." Sam forced himself to hold her gaze, staring her down.

"Maybe. But I tell you what, Sam. Despite what they may have told you at the Academy, you're not the one, great hope to save the world."

"Oh yeah?"

"Not even close," Stella said with certainty in her voice. "You're the one who will enslave it."

17

They landed in Cairo and were met by a team of Enterprise Agents, dressed in their trademark gray suits. Xavier could see that Rapha looked uneasy, perhaps thinking back to whatever he'd been through with Sam in Brazil when rogue Agents were hunting them down. But there was barely any time to reassure him, to tell him to trust these Agents here today, that they were different, they were there to help. There was hardly any time to even think as they were sped through the airport, bundled into beat-up cars and on towards Dr. Kader's workshop at the edge of the city.

Xavier watched out the window, a heavy weight in his stomach. A sense of dread, impending doom. He tried to concentrate on what was happening outside his window.

Cairo.

He'd always loved the hot, bustling, vibrant city on his many visits. It was part of his life, part of his blood. He closed his eyes and thought of his mother, smiling.

But when he opened them, all he could see was the fear swirling in the ancient streets.

In a city of so many, all of them vying for space, for a life, it was a beautiful kind of chaos at the best of times. Now was not the best of times—far from it. He could tell, from the crowds and the chants and the looks on faces that they passed, that the people of Egypt were going through nightmares on a massive scale. Unrest was spilling onto the streets as people seemed to be protesting about everything and demanding answers.

There were pictures of Sam on some signs, while others had slogans. Even walls had been spray painted.

Xavier tried to shut it out. He attempted to listen in as Phoebe made several calls—they were all about Alex and the others in Antarctica, asking for updates, for news, for anything. He could see the worry on her face as she desperately waited to hear about her son, still lost somewhere at the bottom of the world. The others were busy watching the streets outside the windows—soldiers were everywhere, trying to keep everything calm, but even they looked spooked, tired and ready to join the protests.

We all have nightmares, Xavier thought as they drove into the neighborhood where Dr. Kader's home and workshop was tucked away.

No one is immune to them, even the best Dreamers like the Professor still have them.

The cars pulled to a stop. Xavier and the others got out. It was quiet here, deserted.

In this part of the old quarter of town, most of the tiny stores and businesses were closed for the day. Xavier had seen it quiet before, but not like this. Something wasn't right.

On the fifth ring of the doorbell, Phoebe made a call on her phone.

Xavier was nervous.

Where's my father? He looked up and down the street. It was still quiet.

Maybe everyone's in the city center, protesting. Or locked indoors for safety.

He thought of when he was here with Sam, not that long ago.

Today felt different.

Then, it was all unknown, an adventure. Now—now we're so close, and it's as though things might fall apart at any moment.

He couldn't shake the feeling they were being watched. That a group of bad guys—working for Hans, Stella, whoever—would descend upon them and wreak havoc. He looked at the windows of the houses and offices, watching, waiting, expecting to see some kind of menace.

"Xavier," Zara said, standing right next to him.

He jumped.

"Sorry," Zara said. "You are sure that your father is here?"

"He said he would be," Xavier said, ringing the bell yet again.

Cody stood at the edge of their group, looking around. "Wasn't your dad meant to meet us? Fate of the world hanging in the balance and all that? And what—he went out to grab a kebab?"

"You know what, Cody?" Xavier said, aggressively walking towards him. The others intervened as Cody threw his hands up in surrender.

"Yeah, dude," Cody laughed, "I was just kidding around."

"I'm thinking now is not the time for jokes," Poh said.

Xavier turned as he heard footsteps on the other side of Dr. Kader's door.

Two of the Agents drew their dart guns, ready to fire.

The door opened and a man stood there.

"*Dad?*" Xavier said. He almost didn't recognize the man standing in the dark doorway. It *was* his father, he realized, but not as he'd ever seen him. He had the beginnings of a beard, for a start, and he'd never seen his father unshaven. But it was his clothes and all the dust and grime on him that was even more bizarre. He looked like he'd been living on the Cairo streets for weeks—no, not "on" the streets, *under* them.

What happened? I only saw him a few days ago . . .

"Son!" Dr. Dark hugged Xavier, and then looked up and down the street, spooked and concerned. "Quick, inside, all of you—there's no time to lose!"

18

Sam looked at Stella and swallowed hard.

Enslave the world? No chance I'm going to let that happen.

"You see," Stella said, leaning forward into the space between them, "when I use this machine to lead me to the Dream Gate, well, boy, you're going to be sorry you missed what happens after that."

"Your evil plans sound just fascinating but . . ." Sam said quietly, looking at the floor by his feet. "This is going to hurt," he mumbled to himself.

"What was that?" Stella's eyes narrowed as she glared at Sam, leaning forward.

"I said," Sam said, his voice still quiet so that Stella had to get even closer to hear him over the snowcat's engine, "cop *this!*"

Sam head-butted Stella with all the strength he could muster.

His forehead hit her right in the nose.

Stella fell back, clutching at her face, her dart gun clattering to the floor. He snatched it up and fired a dart into her neck without a moment's hesitation. He spun around to the rogue Agent at the back of the snowcat who was rushing towards him—

WHACK! WHACK!

Sam darted him twice.

The driver turned—the situation dawning on him as he grappled to release his seat belt, reaching towards a holster hanging from the opposite seat.

"Don't do it!" Sam commanded him, aiming his dart pistol.

The driver didn't heed Sam's warning. He pulled out the gun, swinging around to aim at Sam.

Sam shot him twice in the arm and he immediately slumped to the floor. As he did, he let go of the steering wheel. And his foot slammed down on the accelerator.

Oh no!

With no time to reach the brakes or steering wheel, Sam threw himself into the nearest seat and pulled his harness on, clicking the straps over his shoulders and into the seat just as the snowcat went out of control, turning hard to the right.

It was turning too hard for their speed. A second later, the treads hit the snow at such a sharp angle that they bit in, stopping them cold.

They flipped and flipped again, rolling sideways at an incredible rate.

Sam felt as if he was inside a giant washing machine. Equipment and the unconscious bodies of Stella and the

Agents tumbled around him, a coil of rope hitting him in the face, an Agent luckily missing him by a hair's breadth as he flew around the cabin like a rag doll.

The snowcat catapulted across the ground, finally coming to a slowing stop, sliding on its side and digging into the ice until it had cut deep enough.

Sam didn't pause for a second. As soon as the snowcat ground to a halt, he made for the rear cargo door, punching the release button. As the ramp hissed open, he unclipped a snow bike and threw his leg over to kick-start the lever and turn over the engine. He pulled on snow goggles and a heavy snowsuit from the rack and tied it around his waist. There was no time to put it on now.

The door ahead opened. He revved hard and shot out into the snow.

The other two snowcats had stopped ahead. Sam didn't bother waiting to see if they turned around to give chase. He sped up, heading away from the scene.

I wish I could rescue you now, Lora, but the odds just aren't on my side.

I know this is what you'd want me to do.

I'll come back for you, I promise.

He knew that she'd understand—in fact, he knew that she'd be mad if he didn't take the chance to make a run for it. Sam grit his teeth and kept the bike speeding along, the chill wind biting into his face. He didn't know if the other vehicles had bikes also, so he wanted to put as much distance between him and them as possible.

Any head start is a good head start.

He followed the tracks of the snowcats back towards Crawley Station.

Eva and the others are there—and I'm betting they're in danger too.

The weather beat Sam to it. A bank of clouds, coming from over the mountains to the east, brought an eerie calm for a few minutes. But then the snow started, and it soon became so intense that he could barely see his feet on the bike let alone the tracks in the snow.

He checked his watch.

Two and a half hours until the super storm hits.

Maybe this is just a front that will pass.

He slowed the bike to a crawl. He tried to make out the deep tracks left by the heavy snowcats, but they'd now been wiped away.

I can't go on, not in this. I could get lost forever.

Sam stopped the bike. He was on flat terrain, the snow already up to his ankles as he got off and pulled on his snowsuit.

Well, I can't see where I'm going—but at least they can't follow me in this.

The back of the bike had a small pack strapped to it. He used the ice ax and his gloved hands to dig into the snow to shield himself from the worst of the freezing wind.

I'm going to have to wait out the worst of it. Soon as I get a bit of a clear patch, I'll head off again. He dug a ditch to hunker down into.

Least we're all in the same boat—Alex won't be finding any Gear in this weather.

19

EVA

Eva walked swiftly down the corridor, cringing as she waited for someone to call out. But the footsteps behind her died away and she realized it must just have been one of the other personnel moving around the base. But as she continued to walk, she heard more noises up ahead.

I'll do a circuit of the whole building—go back the other way.

A man came out of a room ahead of her. He looked at Eva and seemed a little surprised, either by the fact that he'd not seen her before, or that she herself seemed spooked.

Eva smiled, forcing herself to appear calm and at ease, and passed by him, taking the first turn to the left. It was one of the interconnecting corridors, linking the three rings of the main buildings. She walked through the habitat ring and did not pause, just kept going, frantically trying to work out what to do.

They've got to be Stella's Agents. They must have gotten here just before us.

And they've got Arianna and Gabriella!

And that means Sam and Lora are in danger too. I have to get word to them.

But how? I can't go back to the communications room— they'll be there, waiting for me.

Eva entered the inner pod, glancing at the sign above the double doors: MESS HALL.

She pushed through the doors and came into the kitchen and dining room, a space big enough for maybe fifty personnel to sit and eat.

Now there were only two people seated across the room, casually watching a small television screen while playing chess. They noticed Eva. She smiled a nervous smile. They didn't smile back.

Are they station crew, or Stella's Agents? How do I know?

Eva walked slowly over to the kitchen counter and started making a drink. The two guys were silent at their game, stealing glances at her. They even moved their little TV screen so that she couldn't see what was on it.

Maybe this is what happens when you spend too long down here in the snow and ice—you become secretive, wary of outsiders.

Should I approach them? Maybe talk to them, act like I'm on a break, see how they respond? Ask if they know of any backup communications equipment in here so that I can get some kind of warning to Sam and Lora?

Though she couldn't put her finger on why exactly, Eva felt that she had to sit near them. Maybe to find out what they were watching. She took her hot chocolate and a magazine and sat at a booth table behind them. As she went by, she saw the monitor. They were watching somewhere outside, the image white on white with little contrast. They had a radio on the table between them too, like the sort the police use to communicate. Neither of the guys had looked at her.

Maybe I'm reading too much into all this. I should ask them if they've seen Gabriella and Arianna.

She flicked through the magazine, gathering her resolve. Then she heard the radio crackle and a voice said, "Going Stealth. Taking care of the—"

The radio went dead, like it was turned off.

A heavy weight settled in Eva's stomach.

Going Stealth.

So these guys are rogue Agents too.

Taking care of the . . . what?

What do I do now?

One of the guys stood up and sauntered over to the kitchen counter.

Eva picked up her mug and began to walk towards the door at the far side of the mess hall.

Go through the habitat and the work rings, and from there I can get to the exit at the ice runway and the machinery huts.

There must be a radio in one of the spare snowcats. Contact Jedi, warn Sam and Lora.

As she walked to the door, Eva glanced back over her

shoulder to realize in horror that the two guys were closing in on her fast!

Eva threw her scalding hot drink at one and he reeled back.

The other lunged at her but she sidestepped and used his forward momentum to flip him onto his back. He slammed into the corner of one of the metal tables and landed with a thud, out cold.

With one swift movement she grabbed the other Agent, who was still staggering, rubbing his eyes, and pulled him into a choke hold until he too passed out.

Straining and heaving for breath, Eva dragged them, one by one, to a walk-in pantry in the kitchen. She lay them down inside, then she closed the door and wedged a chair under the handle.

"That'll buy me some time," she said. She zigzagged through the scattered tables and chairs to pick up their radio before she raced from the room.

Eva moved quickly through the habitat to the tech ring. Before her was an air lock, one of the four positioned at the points of the compass, the only ways in and out of the base. This was the lock that led to the airstrip and outside pods.

Without a second thought, Eva entered the air lock.

XAVIER

"Ah, didn't you say we had no time to lose?" Xavier whispered to his father.

"Yes," Dr. Dark said. "Just a moment, in a minute. The pyramids are not going anywhere."

"This guy's lost it . . . " Cody whispered to Maria.

Xavier shot Cody a look that showed he'd heard the comment and that he didn't appreciate it. But it was hard to dispute. His father was always dressed immaculately, always appeared so calm and measured, in control.

The man he saw standing before them now had clearly been obsessing over something for days, to the point of not bothering to shower, or change clothes, or even eat.

"And then—*bam!*" Dr. Dark said, pacing the room in front of the assembled last 13 and Phoebe. "It hit me!" He fell silent—there was something he was thinking about. His eyes focused off in the distance. He was either deep in thought or he'd drawn a blank on what to say next.

Maybe my dad has lost it? Working for too many days without sleep.

Sleep deprivation can make people seem crazy, right?

The world's foremost expert dream psychologist certainly looked like he hadn't dreamed in a long, long time. For the first time in his life, Xavier was worried for his father's health and mental state.

I should never have let him leave me in London after we got back from the Ukraine. I should have come here with him, watched over him.

He's all I've got now, we should stick together.

"Kader always said that this location, right here," Dr. Dark tapped his feet on the stone floor to signify he meant the house they were in, "was vital to his research. Vital! And so, I bought it for him almost twenty years ago, and the good doctor has been doing his research not just from here, but *about* here, ever since."

"Wait," Xavier said. "This place—this *building*, is important? To the race?"

"Oh, yes," Dr. Dark said, life returning to his eyes as though a veil of weariness had been lifted. "This, son, you will have to see for yourself."

Xavier had been in the two basement levels before. Originally built for storage, they were packed floor to ceiling with boxes of notes and artifacts that Dr. Kader had collected during his many years of research.

There was barely enough room to move between the

stacks and piles of crates and Zara tripped into his back at one point, causing them all to tread more warily and move things out of their way. His father, Xavier saw, moved through the mayhem like he'd done it a million times.

"Dad . . ." Xavier said, following Dr. Dark down the seemingly never-ending path through the stored artifacts. "You went through all of these boxes?"

"Oh, these? Yes," Dr. Dark said, stopping and looking around as though seeing it all for the first time. "You see, I knew it was in here somewhere. I'd seen it before, years ago. I'll never forget it. And when I dreamed that it was what we needed, I went there, searching for it. A needle in a haystack—a scrap in a notebook, a tiny piece of paper that was somewhere . . ."

"What was it?" Phoebe asked, trying to help him focus. Xavier could see the obvious concern etched on her face.

"A diagram," Dr. Dark replied. "A map, of sorts. Yes, a map. So many maps here. So many to sort through. Hundreds, thousands! But this one was different. Want to see it?"

Xavier nodded.

Dr. Dark pulled a small piece of paper from his shirt pocket. It was creased and yellowed with age.

"Kader made this and showed it to me years ago, Xavier," Dr. Dark said. "He made it but I don't think even he realized the significance."

"What *is* it?" Xavier asked. They were all crowded around, trying to make sense of what looked like the world's biggest maze.

"A map," Dr. Dark said, matter-of-fact.

"Dad, you've said that," Xavier said, his hand on his father's. "But a map of *what*, and *where?*"

"Oh, right, of course, you don't know," Dr. Dark said, his eyes turning to the old steel door at the end of the subbasement.

Xavier knew the door, he'd seen it hundreds of times. But he'd never been through it. Dangerous—very dangerous, Ahmed had always told him. When pressed, he had said it led to a water cistern under the street, that the area had once used as its water well. Xavier had always wondered if there was more to it.

"Stars falling underground . . ." Dr. Dark said quietly.

"Sorry?" Xavier asked. "Dad, what did you say?"

"Stars. The stars are falling . . ."

"Dad—when did you last sleep?"

"Sleep?" He took Xavier by the shoulders and looked into his eyes. "Xavier—there's no time to sleep, not now!"

"The stars?" Xavier said to his father in an even tone. "And the moon? Is this about the thirteenth moon?"

"Thirteen, yes . . . unlucky for all sorts of reasons, mainly to hide the significance, so that we would not think about it."

Dr. Dark turned from the group and walked down to the door. Xavier looked to the others. Their faces betrayed expressions of varying degrees of concern and confusion.

Xavier signaled for them to stay put, then he joined his father at the end of the basement.

It was just him and his dad, standing by the door.

"Dad . . ."

Dr. Dark turned to face Xavier.

"You need rest. You're tired."

Dr. Dark nodded. "You're right. But we're here now, so close. We can be the ones, son. In a few short days, we can be at the Dream Gate, do you understand? My whole life, I've waited for this. My father's whole life. Entire generations of Darks."

"I know," Xavier said. "Tell me—what do you mean about the stars? What's that map? What's beyond that door?"

"Well . . ." Dr. Dark said, looking from his son to the door as he said, "we'll have to go under the pyramids to show you."

SAM

Sam took shelter in his makeshift snow cave. It certainly wasn't warm, but the wind was blocked out and his own warmth was trapped around him.

Man, I'm so tired. What's with me?

Well, I guess I haven't had a good night's sleep since . . . huh. A while.

Gotta stay awake.

He opened his backpack, which had been packed by Jabari on the flight there. He rifled through the contents—one flashlight and a head-mounted flashlight, which he was now wearing, an ice ax for digging and climbing. There were two ration packs, each a plastic bag the size of a couple of bricks stacked together.

He cracked one open. It contained packages of food in smaller plastic bags. He ate cheese and crackers, a fruit bar and then drank a juice. He pushed his backpack to the entrance of his little dugout to form a door, and rolled onto his back, the hood of his snowsuit a warm pillow. He checked his watch.

Just over two hours until the storm hits in full.

Feels like the wind's dying down ahead of the storm.
I'll give it another ten minutes and start moving again.
Just a little rest.
Sam closed his eyes against the wind and the cold.

SAM'S NIGHTMARE

I am in an apartment. I stand at a floor-to-ceiling window, the whole wall made up of thick glass. I look out at the view. I see a big city, unrecognizable yet familiar, like it is made up of parts of the cities I've visited these past months. The sun is setting.

"See it?" Eva says.

I look to my left and see that she's standing next to me. She's looking up at the sky. I look too. I see the sunlight reflecting off something. An aircraft, but an odd one . . .

A blimp.

With an electronic sign.

I squint to read it, shielding the sun from my eyes.

Thanks, Sam—you're our hero!

A picture of my face fills the screen.

Sam saved us! flashes up the next slogan.

Now it shows a picture of me in action.

Thank you, Sam!

A picture of me as a kid.

Great.

"What's that about?" I ask.

"You did it," Eva says. "It's over."

"Did it?"

"Won the race."

"Oh." I look again at the sign. "*We* did it. *Thirteen* of us together, right?"

"If you say so."

I look to Eva. "What?" I ask.

She looks past me, over my shoulder.

I turn. Alex is there.

"Hey!" I say. "I was looking for you." I pause. "Not here though. I needed to find you . . ."

Alex remains silent, then he faces the window.

"I'm not here," Alex says.

"Figured as much," I reply. The three of us stand there, the remains of the daylight a warm orange glow against our faces. "But I need to find you. Fast. There's a storm coming. And, well, you know . . . the usual bad guys."

"Then look for me," Alex says. "Can't be hard."

"Ah, it is hard. I'm trying."

"*Are you?*"

"I think so."

"Then you're looking in the wrong place. We're in the future. You need to look in the now."

"Easier said than done . . ."

Alex points. "What do you see out here?"

I lean forward, searching.

"Sometimes you have to fall," Alex says, "before you can really get to where you need to be."

"I know," I say.

"Then fall."

"Where?"

"With us," Eva says.

The glass gives way, simply vanishes, and the three of us, holding hands, fall through the air towards the ground below.

I've never felt so free.

But this is not where I'm meant to be. What's Alex really telling me? Where is he?

I hit the ground, I close my eyes and drift . . .

SAM

Sam was jolted awake by something moving.

Oh no! How long have I been asleep?

There was a rumbling sound. It wasn't him moving, it was the *ground*.

He knelt up to get free of his snow shelter but the snow was frozen in place. He kicked at it and used his small ice ax to smash his way through. The sky was gray, but there was water too.

Water?

He scrambled onto his hands and knees and got to his feet. He slung his backpack over his shoulder and gazed at the view. Before him was the ocean. It was a long, long way down. But it was slowly getting closer.

I'm standing right on the edge of an ice shelf.

A very tall ice shelf.

And it's carving off the continent in a massive, slow-moving avalanche!

Sam spun around in a circle to get his bearings. Already the ground beneath him, hundreds of feet of solid ice, was tilting towards the ocean. He turned inland and broke into a sprint.

As he fled, a noise reverberated through the air and Sam's fear choked him—it was the sound of millions of tons of ice shearing off from the mainland, destined to hit the freezing water, where it would break up to form thousands of icebergs that would drift out to sea.

Ahead of Sam, the ground tilted further and further into an incline, so it felt as though he was running up a drawbridge as it was being raised.

Gotta make it! Gotta hustle!

Sam hustled.

When the edge was just in front—he jumped.

And he nearly made it.

Sam swung the ice ax out and it bit into the hard snow. Both hands on the ax, he looked through his dangling feet.

Sam was hanging on for his life.

And beneath his feet was a nine-hundred-foot drop into

the freezing sea. Waves pounded the ice. Car-sized pieces of the cliff face were tearing off with great creaks and cracks, smashing into the churning sea below.

Don't fall, don't fall . . .

EVA

*G*oing outside might have been a bad idea.

The wind was the worst thing about being outside. It blew with such force, and at such an angle, that Eva had to walk into it headfirst, leaning forward with all her weight.

The snowsuit she'd taken from the air lock belonged to a staffer about three sizes bigger than her. That hadn't mattered when she had put it on, but it now meant that it was acting like a sail. Every two steps forward she was pushed one step back towards the base. And those steps were slow, slow going.

Even Mother Nature thinks this is a bad idea.

But Eva persisted. She walked towards one of the large buildings she'd seen on her way in, next to where they'd touched down.

It took ten minutes to get there, ten minutes to walk what would have taken her two minutes in good weather.

Briony will probably be doing her fifteen-minute visit about now.

Eva stopped at the wall of the structure and stood

there to catch her breath, shielded from most of the wind by the building.

Where's the door?

With the snow whipping through the air, she felt around the building with her hands, fumbling around as if in the dark. That took her another two minutes.

Useless.

The door was locked with a big, shiny padlock on the door. The radio in her hand crackled—something about a "check-in" but she couldn't be sure. Eva nearly completed a full circuit of the building when she stopped at a frosted-over window that was fogged up on the inside. She wiped off the snow and could just make out another snowcat inside.

I could use that radio to contact Lora.

The handheld radio crackled again but against the wind it was too noisy to hear anything. Eva looked at the radio in her hands.

Why not?

She stood side-on, took a big swing and used the handset to smash the window.

Eva cleared the glass off with the radio and tossed that through first, then hauled herself through the opening, landing with a thump.

She got to her feet and looked around. Inside, there were two snowcats and a large snowplow.

And there was something else.

People.

The first thing Eva did was to untie her friends, Arianna and Gabriella.

They were panicked and pleased at the same time, and told a rapid-fire version of how they had been trapped out there by two of the men at the base.

"Quickly!" Gabriella said. "They'll be back any minute!"

"No, they won't," Eva said, thinking of the men she'd left unconscious and trapped in the pantry. "Help me untie the others."

All around them sat a dozen other people, all tied and gagged—the *real* Crawley Station crew. The three of them began untying the prisoners as quickly as they could.

"It was Briony," Gabriella said. "She and the two guys forced us in here at gunpoint." She hesitated, her eyes filling with tears. "I think they killed Harry and Larry."

"Oh my . . ." Eva was at a loss for words. She felt overwhelmed at the thought of more brave Guardians losing their lives. She felt the color drain from her face as she looked at Gabriella and Arianna.

"Eva?" Arianna said gently. "We need you now. You must stay strong."

"Who *are* these people?" Gabriella asked.

"Stella's gang," Eva said, standing up and watching as the rest of the crew untied each other. "Gotta be, they're the only others at play now—Mac's gone, and Hans and his guys were, or *are*, with Alex."

A small man with thick glasses came up to Eva.

"Thank you," he said to her. "I'm Dr. Roberts. We've been tied up in here since last night. They only left a small gas heater for us. I thought . . . another night in here, and I thought we were done for."

"You're welcome, it's the least we could do," Eva replied. "I'm so sorry you've been caught up in this. But tell me, do the radios in the 'cats work?"

Dr. Roberts shook his head. "They wrecked them," he replied.

"We have to leave," Eva said. "We have to warn our friends."

"The Chilean and Chinese stations are about fifty miles southeast of here. They'll have radios."

"Can you take us?"

"One of us can drive you there," he said. "But what are—"

CLONG!

There was a loud bang on the door. Eva ran over. She used her sleeve to clear the frosted condensation from the glass porthole in the steel door. Outside the tiny window she spotted Briony, along with three of her guys, all armed. She pointed left and right and the guys fanned out.

"What are they doing?" Dr. Roberts asked, joining her.

"Surrounding us," Eva said.

"What do we do?" Gabriella asked. "What *can* we do?"

"We have to help Sam," Eva said. "No matter what. Get a warning to him."

"But he's already two hours away."

"Then we've got no time to lose."

"Maybe they've already told Stella that they've got us all trapped in here."

"I don't think so," Eva said, leaving the door and walking around, checking out the equipment that was wrapped up against the cold. "Briony will try to deal with this herself first. I don't think anyone working for Stella wants to give her anything but good news."

"OK, but what can we do?" Arianna said.

"Sir, can we assist?"

They turned to find four men standing in a group.

"These men are military scientists," Dr. Roberts said. "They're a bit more used to this than the rest of us."

Looking around, Eva could see most of the crew looked incredibly frightened.

I don't blame them.

Fortunately, the real Dr. Roberts was a born leader. "Right, we can't leave anyone here with these thugs outside. Kyle," he said to the closest man, "I want one of your men to drive these girls to the Chilean base in one 'cat, and we'll take the rest of the crew in the other."

"Yes, sir," Kyle said, his men snapping into action, ushering the scared crew into a vehicle.

"We're going to need to create a diversion," Kyle said,

looking to the equipment in the garage. "I can blast out the door with the snowplow. We can improvise some weapons—Bob, rig that gas tank to toss and blow."

"You got it, chief," Bob replied. Eva watched a huge guy start to disassemble the heater and turn it into a makeshift bomb.

OK, loving having scientists and soldiers on our side.

"Follow the compass on the snowcat," Dr. Roberts told them. "Due southeast, fifty miles, you'll see the small Chinese station first, try there. If there's no one there now and it's locked up, the Chilean base is about five more miles east of it and is manned all year round. Got it? Pete here will drive you and he's a good guy."

"Thank you," Eva said, shaking the man's hand.

"No problem, miss," Pete said. "Let's get out of here."

The rest of the Crawley Station crew were now all in the other snowcat, trying to lie low for safety.

"Good luck," Dr. Roberts said and closed the snowcat's door.

Eva turned to her friends. "Time to buckle up."

XAVIER

There was silence in the group. Xavier looked at his father. They all looked at him, waiting for further explanation. But none came.

"Funny," Cody said, breaking that silence and laughing nervously. "I thought you said *under* the pyramids—like right *underneath* them. Ha-ha."

"That's right," Dr. Dark said, "I did."

The others had joined them at the steel door.

"What did you find through there?" Xavier asked, pointing to the door. "Is it that maze?"

"I want to show you," Dr. Dark said. "You're all here . . . and every moment counts. This is a race—we should press on, get ahead while we can."

Xavier tried to read his father's eyes, to see if he had really cracked under the pressure. His expression was unfamiliar to Xavier, he didn't know *what* to make of it.

"Wait a sec—you really mean 'under the pyramids'?" Xavier said. "Like deep underground?"

Dr. Dark nodded.

"OK . . ." Xavier said.

That's it—my dad has completely lost it. There's nothing under the pyramids. The world would have known by now if there was.

"Herodotus, the Greek historian," Phoebe said, trying to calm the group, "he visited Egypt in the fifth century BCE. He told a story about vaults under the pyramids, built on an island."

"That was my first thought too," Dr. Dark said. "So I had to look."

"Let's do it, then," Phoebe said to Dr. Dark. "Show us what you've found."

Xavier looked back at the open steel door, now only a tiny dot of light behind them. They found their way by their flashlights and a couple of old oil lanterns that Dr. Dark had lit.

Under Dr. Kader's building, a cavern with stairs carved into the limestone led to a water source.

"So Ahmed was telling me the truth," Xavier said, standing by the edge of the water and putting his hand in. It was cold and fast moving, a little underground river. "This *was* a water supply for the old city."

"Probably one of many," Phoebe said. "Deserts are only dry on the surface. There's always water—if you go deep enough."

"This is neat," Cody said, tasting the water. "I mean—kinda awesome. It's so fresh, drinkable. But I don't get it." He stood up, shining his light overhead. "An underground water table is cool but it's not that big a deal. I didn't see anything else on our way down here. Just a few doors—other basements, I guess."

"No," Dr. Dark said. "That's not true. If you care to look, if you are patient, you will find a way."

Cody did another sweep with his light and shrugged.

"The water," Xavier said, looking from it to his father, "does it flow into the Nile?"

"Some of it," his father said. "Some to a big aqueduct. I believe it is also channeled off to other areas."

"Channeled off?" Xavier said.

"This is like an ancient plumbing system," Phoebe called over, from a section of wall with small tunnels carved into it. "This isn't just a naturally occurring water supply. It's been fashioned to provide water elsewhere."

Dr. Dark nodded.

"I followed them," he said. "All those tunnels that they made. See?"

He led them over to where Phoebe stood. The arched tunnels, next to each other, were almost big enough to stand up in—and were clearly man-made. The water running into them was ankle deep and clear.

"See?"

He shone his flashlight at one particular tunnel, staring

at it. At first there didn't seem to be anything special about it until they looked at a marking above the arch. It was an engraving, in Roman numerals.

Dr. Dark went into the tunnel.

"The Roman Empire conquered Ancient Egypt," Phoebe said, following in a crouch behind Xavier who was behind his father. The others walked in single file through the tunnel. "They must have built these tunnels to carry the water, just like the aqueducts they built in all their territories."

"The Romans just fixed it up," Dr. Dark said over his shoulder. "It's older than Rome."

Xavier knew not to question his father's knowledge— he must have looked at the construction and made his assessment based on that. He knew Ancient Egypt better than most.

"How far are we going?" Xavier asked after they'd traveled for twenty minutes through the single, straight tunnel, not a maze in sight.

"Just up here," Dr. Dark said. "A little further."

24

SAM

Sam's arms screamed in agony as he clung to the ax. He tried to pull himself up further, but his arms were too stiff from the cold. Gingerly, he pried one hand from the ax, using the free hand to cling to the ground that was now a wall of ice.

I can't hold on much longer. How can I climb up?

There was a thunderous crack below him and suddenly the wall of ice started tipping back, righting itself horizontal once more.

The ice must have split in half!

With renewed strength, Sam crouched in, ready to sprint. As soon as the ground came back to a lower angle, he sprang forward, flinging himself over to reach safer ground. Just before him, he saw the edge of the broken land, the chasm widening as the ice pulled away from the mainland.

Sam threw himself across, not daring to glance down, and tumbled head over heels as he cleared the gap and landed on solid earth. But he did not stop there, picking himself up to run at a quick jog, putting distance between him and the falling ice sheet.

Man!

Finally he risked stopping, doubling over with his hands on his knees, sucking in breath as his heart rate struggled to slow. He looked out to the sea behind him, already swallowing up the broken ice.

"Wrong . . . place . . . to make camp."

Sam straightened up to get his bearings, catching sight of the mountains to the east. He took a deep breath and set off, running into the ever-increasing wind.

Sam was starting to really worry.

He only had one ration pack left. He remembered the survival briefing from Jabari on the flight there.

I'd need like a lot, a million calories, to survive in the elements. A billion calories if I was doing physical work, like traversing the frozen ground.

His stomach rumbled. He packed up the little chemical heater that had thawed out a thermos of water, to which he'd added coffee and sweetened milk, had a gulp, leaving it about half full, then tucked the warm thermos under his snowsuit at the front to keep his chest warm. He packed away his equipment and strapped the pack on tight over his shoulders.

Then there was the weather. But it was clear now and the wind had died down.

Too quiet.

Sunlight hit the mountains and fingers of clouds stretched over them, as though reaching for him. The sun was low to the west. It would still be hours before it set. And it was only gone for a few hours at the most at this time of year.

"C'mon, Sam, you can make it another hour," he said, goading himself on as he trudged, his boots biting into the ice, the sun warming his face. "Another hour, you'll find . . . something. I hope."

The hour to make camp never came.

Sam stopped to listen.

There was a noise, in the distance.

He turned around and around, looking for its source.

Am I really hearing that?

Sounds like a . . . machine? A truck?

The wind had picked up. It brought more clouds with it, and worse, the ice crystals from the frozen ground blasted against his face. He had the Stealth Suit inside his snowsuit and had it formed as a full-face balaclava, his goggles protecting his eyes. But the ice still stung. And the wind still blew, stronger than ever, so that for every five steps forward he felt he was being swept a step back. His legs burned and his stomach grumbled.

But the noise . . .

Sam crouched into a ball, his back to the wind, and listened.

Is it just the wind?

The sky darkened.

WHOOSH!

A shape blasted overhead—large and warm.

Sam stood and waved. It was a jet. It passed over him, without ever seeing him. But as he watched, he tripped and fell. His head smashed into the ground as the plane passed out of sight.

SAM'S NIGHTMARE

"You won't burn me," I say.

"No?"

"You've taken so many shots and done nothing but singe my Stealth Suit. You wouldn't kill me."

"No, I wouldn't. But you're afraid of fire. And you *should* be."

"But you won't kill me."

"No. But there are things worse than death."

"Who were you?" I ask. "Before you put that suit on— who were you?"

"Sam, you're about to learn why thirteen is an unlucky number—"

SAM

Sam's watch alarm bleeped and he came to with a start.

Oh no!

He looked at the little screen.

00:00:00

Countdown over.

But no storm.

Maybe they were wrong about the weather? Maybe it passed around us, or dissipated?

He looked around. The day seemed fine. Clear skies as far as he could see in all directions.

The mountains to the east . . . are disappearing!

What the . . . ?

A wall of white was moving across the mountains and rushing over the ice. It was like all the snow in the world was being drawn into that storm.

Sam jumped up and ran.

The Chilean station, that's the closest. Find it, Sam, find it!

ALEX

Alex looked down from the top of the pyramid.

It's not often you get to climb one of these. OK, well, unless you're Sam or Xavier.

No guards to tell me off here, though.

The solid chamber around them was easily the size of the biggest sports stadium he'd ever seen.

A pyramid built inside a mountain . . . but where's my Gear? In my dream it was like I had already found it.

Have I changed too much of the lead up, so that meeting Sam like that will never happen?

"It's through here!" Ahmed called.

Alex followed the bright lights to where Hans stood with Dr. Kader.

At the opening to the pyramid, Alex paused. Hans and Ahmed looked at him.

"What is it?" Hans asked.

"This—this place," Alex said, looking around him at the door. "It's familiar. It's the dream that I just told you about. This is it."

"Good!" Hans said. "Now, the Gear—do you remember where the Gear is?"

He closed his eyes, concentrating . . . standing right there was the strangest kind of déjà vu and Alex could feel the recollection of his dream flickering tantalizingly just out of reach of his mind.

"Anything?" Ahmed said.

"Shhh," Alex said, not opening his eyes. "I need to let my mind drift back to that part of the dream."

"Take all the time you need," Hans said. "I've waited this long, I can wait a few minutes longer."

Yeah, but you're going to be waiting longer than that.

No way I'm just handing my Gear over to you. No matter how much fun we've had on your boat.

Alex sat down, leaning against the cool stones of the pyramid, trying to let his mind flow naturally.

If I force it, I won't see it.

He could hear Ahmed shifting from foot to foot but Hans was silent . . . *like a snake.*

What happens when I find it?

Stop it, Alex! Concentrate on the Gear first.

He refocused his mind, picturing himself holding a Gear . . . minutes ticked by.

"It was hidden behind a wall," Alex said suddenly, leaping up and startling both Ahmed and Hans.

They walked down the stairs and then down the pyramid corridor to a sheer rock wall at the very back.

"It's there, I think. No, I'm sure," Alex said. "But we'll need to dig it out."

"Good enough for me," Hans replied. "And I have men for that." As they came back outside the pyramid, Hans clicked his fingers and his men came running.

"Are these . . . hieroglyphics?" Alex asked, pointing to carvings as they walked around the cavern, waiting for Hans' men to break through the wall. "Even within the room here, not just the pyramid?"

"Yes," Ahmed said. "A different form of them."

"Egyptian, though?"

"Some similarities, but no, not Egyptian. These are earlier."

"Earlier . . ." Alex's awe at the sight was interrupted by the sound of a rumbling explosion. He turned back to the pyramid in time to see Hans' men standing next to a cloud of dust.

"They're through!" Hans said, clapping his hands together.

"Yes," Ahmed said. "Though I'm not sure that they *should* go through."

"Why?" Alex asked.

Ahmed looked at Alex. "Some doors are meant to remain closed."

Alex ran forward, nervous and excited to finally see his Gear, his part of the machine—of the race itself. But before he could reach the pyramid, there was a noise like the world was tearing apart.

"The explosives!" Ahmed said. "They've opened up cracks in the lava field!"

Alex immediately saw what he meant.

Steaming lava had started bubbling up all over the floor of the cavern.

"We don't have much time," Hans said. "Hurry!"

26

SAM

The scene ahead seemed like a mirage.

The hood down over his face, the wind threatening to blow him off his feet, Sam stopped and wiped the ice from his goggles.

Is that . . . ?

Yes.

A wooden hut, leaning at an awkward angle, presumably from the wind buffeting it, crates and oil drums all around forming barriers that were banked with drift snow.

It's not the Chilean station, but any port in a storm!

He looked over his shoulder—the wall of wind and snow of the super storm was now just a couple of minutes behind him.

Sam pushed on, the wind at his back, struggling to stay upright with every step as the wind carried him onward. He hit the bank of snow at a row of oil drums and tumbled over it. He crawled to the hut. It was completely made from wood, and though he could not feel it with his double-gloved hands, he could see the wood was blasted smooth, and worn by decades of ice crystals. It felt like it took an eternity to find the door, located on the side opposite the prevailing wind.

It was locked.

He tried to shoulder it, charging at it twice, but it held, the wood thick and strong.

There were no windows.

Maybe I can crash through the wall where it's thinner and weaker, on the other side—

The door flew open.

Two people stood there, brandishing snow axes, ready to strike.

Then, one of them, a woman, lowered her ax and said in shocked disbelief, "Sam?"

Sam gradually thawed out by the fire. It gave the only light in the hut, but it was enough to see his two companions by. A man and a woman, in their thirties—Clive and Nora. They were a news crew, out of New Zealand, there to film a reenactment of a race to the South Pole.

There were eight dogs too. Sled dogs, malamutes, like he'd seen race a few times back in Canada, in the Far North. The leader of the pack was dark gray with a black mane and big eyes. Called River, he sniffed Sam and allowed him to pat his head.

"He's bigger than me," Sam said, motioning to River.

"Yeah, but he's just a big puppy at heart," Nora said.

River licked Sam's face as he laughed. Content that Sam was a friend, River went and sat with the other dogs in the corner of the hut.

Clive went to get more firewood from the adjoining storeroom.

"They don't mind being outside," Sam said to Nora, motioning to the dogs. "They're used to it—it's what they know, what they were bred for."

"I know," Nora replied. "But I just couldn't—not if this storm's going to be as bad as they say. I'd go out tomorrow to find eight dog popsicles."

"Right . . ." Sam said.

Clive dumped a huge pile of former supply crates, now broken up for firewood, in the rusted cast-iron stove that sat squat in the center of the hut. "You're him, aren't you?" he said. "You're that one whose dreams are coming true."

Sam nodded.

"We saw you speak at the UN," Nora said. "You warned the world about some race to control the dream world."

"Yep, that's me," Sam said, holding a hot drink in his hands, the warmth rising up to his face. "Sam the Dreamer . . ."

"A dream led you down here?" Nora asked.

Sam nodded. "It did. I have to find a friend who's down here, looking for something. So I'm still in the news?" he said, changing the subject.

"Every day," Nora said. "Yesterday they interviewed some guy, some kind of academic-looking older man."

Sam laughed. "That'd be the Professor."

"You're not alone in this, Sam," Nora said. "The whole world is waiting, watching."

"I just have to get out of here, keep heading east, to catch up with my friends," Sam said.

"Well, the storm's about to get a lot worse," Clive said. "No one will be able to get to us, not until it passes."

He could see that they only had food packs for two people for a day. And the dogs had nothing but a large tub of dry food. River looked like he could eat it all in two minutes flat if given the chance. The heat of the interior was almost painful after the frigid cold. Sam shook off his gloves, then unzipped his snowsuit and threw back his hood. He rubbed his nose and cheeks to make sure they were still there.

Do you know when you're getting frostbite?

"How'd you guys get to be here, in this hut, I mean?" Sam asked.

"We were here to make a documentary about some New Zealand explorations," Nora said. "Then we heard a rumor." She fell silent, watching the fire, and finally went on. "From Lake Vostok. Then before we knew it, we got diverted by our bosses to cover another related news story."

"News—in Antarctica?" Sam said. "What, they found out that penguins are really wearing tuxedos?"

Clive laughed and passed around more cups of sweet, steaming hot chocolate from a pot above the stove. Sam took one gratefully.

"They found something at Vostok," Nora said. "Drilling down, they brought up stone and metal. They said it was evidence of some kind of spectacular ruins, *underneath* the ice."

"Ruins?" Sam said. "Like, from an early expedition down here?"

"You could put it that way," Clive said. "Though not any expedition you'd read about in the history books. This one was said to be, ah, just a *little* earlier."

"Thousands of years earlier," Nora said, "going by what they found near the Chilean station. They were coring too, so they set their drill to the same depth as at Vostok. The whole drill rig fell through the ice, into some kind of tunnel system."

"The things I've seen these past few months," Sam said, "I'm about ready to believe anything."

"Yeah, we've heard, and read," Nora said. "It seems intense. Maybe we can help, Sam."

"Thank you," Sam said.

"There's plenty of support for you, Sam," Nora said, smiling. "You should check out social media sometime."

"Or switch on the TV," Clive added.

Sam smiled, lost in the thought of having the luxury to do that.

Would it be wrong, reading about myself like that? Maybe not—maybe I need to see and hear that there are people out there cheering us on.

"So you didn't find anything?" Sam said. "In these ruins?"

The pair shared a look.

"Well . . ." Clive began.

"We chalked it up to some kind of sub-zero-induced delusion, you know these guys are out here for months at a time," Nora said, "but when we turned up at the site, we were chased off by soldiers."

"*Whose* soldiers?" Sam asked.

"Whatever big company it is that's paying for the drilling," Clive said. "We're still trying to find out who that is exactly. These kind of businesses hide behind subsidiaries that can take weeks to untangle."

"But why would they chase you off?"

"Because they found something, and they're protecting it while they explore it."

"Our bureau in Auckland got a tip-off that someone down here was willing to talk. We got our guides to go so we could wait here for them in secret. But they haven't shown up. We were planning to leave tomorrow."

"Tomorrow's too late . . ." Sam said, then sat forward. "This place—is it far from here?"

Clive grinned. "It'd be worth the trip."

Then the storm hit.

27

XAVIER

"Dr. Dark," Poh called from behind them as they walked through the tunnel at a crouch. "What do you think will happen, at the Dream Gate?"

Dr. Dark took his time answering.

"Dad?" Xavier said, pausing, and the convoy came to a halt, the tight tunnel making it hard for them all to see each other.

"Just up here, a little more," Dr. Dark replied, turning to smile at them. "Then we'll stop. You'll see."

They walked on and came to a larger space that opened up even further.

A big cistern? Xavier guessed. A place where the water once flowed high, according to the marks on the wall. Now, there was just a trickle of water running through the channel carved into the rock long ago.

"Are they . . . human?" Maria asked, pointing at piles of old bones scattered along the far wall.

"Animal," Rapha said, shining his flashlight over there.

"The Dream Gate," Phoebe gently reminded Dr. Dark. She crouched down to the water and washed her hands in it. "What do you think, Dark? Do you know what we'll find?"

"I believe," Dr. Dark replied, shining his flashlight over the ceiling, "that this ultimate power has something to do with the sun, given the name da Vinci gave his machine."

"The sun?" Xavier said. "I read that Bakhu was the name of a mythical mountain in Ancient Egypt. They believed the sun rose from behind it, right?"

"I'm pleased to see you taking an interest, my son," Dr. Dark said. "Yes, it was one of two great mountains that held up the sky, the other called Manu."

"Sunrise, sunset . . ." Xavier said. "Opposites."

"That's right," Dr. Dark replied. "Light and dark. Life and death. I fear that if the person who enters the Dream Gate is not true—if the power falls into the wrong hands, then we could all be in a world where night is eternal. Darkness will reign. Nightmares will be real."

"You make it sound like a curse," Maria whispered.

"It may well be," Dr. Dark said. "I think there's a good reason that the Dream Gate was hidden away and that finding it is such a battle. We've not been ready, not since the time of Ramses the Great, who sealed the Gate. Not until now, not until the thirteen of you."

"This sounds like a myth to me," Cody said. "The machine is named after a mountain where the sun rose? So you think maybe the holder of this power will, what, control the sun?"

Dr. Dark shook his head. "It's no more unbelievable a story than that of the last 13," he replied. "Which was told to me by my father, and his father to him before that. And here I am—seeing it play out."

"He's right," Phoebe said. "I was told similar stories. About what the ultimate power might be and about the last 13."

"Maybe it was seen as a power way back then—but it's not a power now," Maria said. "Like it has something to do with the stars, or the sky?"

"It could well be something like that," Phoebe said. "You're right."

Dr. Dark nodded. "Everything is connected. Us, the earth, the stars in the sky. Some things are too big to easily explain. But our time is coming, when we are about to find something that has been hidden away from us for well over three thousand years."

SAM

It had howled outside for long hours. The dogs were quiet and still. The three people inside were spooked.

Sam examined the map. Vostok was too far away.

My best bet is the Chilean station.

"The Chilean station," Sam said, tapping the map. "I have to get there as soon as I can."

"In that storm?" Clive said. "It will take too long to get there—you'll freeze."

"It does seem like the storm has died down a bit," Nora said. "We might be OK to wait it out here. You're welcome to stay here with us."

"Thank you," Sam said, "but I really do have to leave. I just can't sit here when there's so little time left."

"Are we running out of time?" Clive said.

"Well, I'm not really free to tell you much more than that right now," Sam said, "but give me a call once it's all over and I'll give you guys an exclusive."

Nora and Clive grinned. "We'll hold you to that," she said. "But I'm still worried about you leaving. It'll take hours to hike there."

"I'm not planning on hiking," Sam said, an idea forming in his mind as he glanced around the hut. "I'm going to get there faster."

"Faster?" she asked. "How?"

"In something I saw outside," Sam said, thinking back to the junk pile. "There's enough here to get me where I need to go."

He saw them look at him in puzzlement.

"I don't get it," Nora said. "And Sam—this weather . . ."

I'm more worried about this hut weathering the storm . . . but I guess it's survived this long.

Sam saw the names of travelers who'd passed through carved into the walls. He used the point of his ice ax to put "SAM of the last 13" on the back of the door.

"OK," he said. "Time to go sailing."

"Thanks for everything," Sam said to the reporting crew.

"You sure we can't do more?" Clive said. "Go with you?"

"You've done more than enough," Sam replied. "You were quite literally my safe harbor in a storm! I'll never forget that. Thank you."

She ain't pretty, Sam thought, as he settled into the old oil-drum craft with rope tethering him to it.

"You call that sailing?" Nora called out over the wind. "You sure you know what you're doing?"

"Ice sailing!" Sam called back. But this was far removed from any kind of sailing Sam had done before. "It'll work, you'll see." He wished he felt as confident as he sounded. This had seemed like a good idea from the warmth of the hut.

Wind filled the nine-foot sail, spreading out a dark green sheet above him. In its previous life, it had been a tarp covering crates, but it was up to this task too.

As for the craft, well . . . could be better. But it could have been worse.

The steel drum's bottom was smooth and sleek and it skidded on the ice, bucking and ready to go. Sam held on tight, his padded snowsuit jamming him in like a sardine.

"Actually, not that uncomfortable!" Sam yelled. "Bye, guys!"

He pulled out his survival knife and cut the rope holding his makeshift boat to the hut. The ice sailer flew away across the frozen ground, the "sail" billowing out, catching the immense wind. In just a few seconds, he was traveling at breathtaking speed.

Sam gripped the knife in his hand. He might need to cut his sail loose if there was a serious obstacle ahead.

What if I just need to slow down? Hmm.

He wiped ice and snow from his goggles.

I ditch the sail.

And what if the wind changes—and I have to alter course?

I ditch the sail.

Sam relaxed as much as he could, watching the endless snow flash past him. Every now and then he'd hit a bump where the snow had formed a ridge or the ice had shifted, and the craft took flight. Sometimes it stayed airborne like that for a few seconds, flying forward, before coming back down to the ground, the jarring return to earth unkind to Sam's body.

Ow. Where's the cushioning in this thing?

He checked his compass, pulling more on the left-hand rope. He glanced across at the blue mountains that rose up to the east.

There is surely no place more empty and barren . . . a desert, maybe.

But this is a frozen desert, just as harsh, and probably even more dangerous.

Even without a super storm, if the cold here didn't get you with frostbite or hypothermia, the terrain would. Sam's greatest fear was that by the time he might spot a huge crevasse and cut the lines to stop—it would be too late.

The momentum would carry me on. Newton's law, right? I'd be swallowed up and never seen or heard from again.

He was really traveling with the wind now, the drum barely touching the ground. Then the wind shifted ever so slightly. Ice kicked up from the front of the craft and covered Sam's goggles. He wiped them clear. The dance of blowing snow started to overtake him as the wind grew in strength.

Is Alex out there? Has he found the Gear yet?

He hit a jagged peak of a ridge—and shot into the air. But this was no ordinary ridge like those he'd hit before. This was a shift in the ice shelf and the plateau ahead was lower.

A lot lower.

Oh boy . . .

Sam could see ahead as the nose of the drum started to drop. Then the wind in the sail picked up and pulled—and he shot upward, a few feet clear of the ground.

And now I'm flying.

Then Sam saw the land ahead. It wasn't another flat, smooth ice run.

It's a field of crevasses!

Sam ditched the sail.

EVA

"**H**old on!" Pete yelled as the snowplow in front of them smashed through the wooden wall of the shed, debris catapulting in all directions as it roared out into the snow.

Peeking above the rim of the window, Eva spotted Briony flat on her back, blown over by the force of Bob's "bomb."

But no sooner were they racing out of the smashed wall at full throttle than Eva heard gunshots and the sound of bullets hitting the side of the vehicle.

"Everyone down!" yelled Pete, his foot to the floor as he crouched behind the wheel.

Eva clung to Arianna and Gabriella as they flattened themselves on the floor of the snowcat, bouncing madly as they made their escape.

A few moments later, Eva dared to lift her head—they were clear of the base, away from Stella's Agents, only whiteness ahead of them. She spun around to look out the back door. The other snowcat was not far behind them.

Thank goodness we got everyone out of there.

Now we have to find Sam and Alex before those guys find us again.

She went up to sit next to Pete. "You OK?" she asked. "Are you hurt?" She panicked at the sight of blood on his face.

"Just a scratch," he said. "Banged my head as we were hotfooting it out of there. I'll get us there soon, don't worry."

"Lora?" Eva said. She couldn't believe her eyes. They had driven into the Chinese base and seen a group of figures arriving on foot. It was Lora, with a Guardian and an Agent.

Eva jumped down and ran over to Lora to hug her. "Stella's Agents took over Crawley Station," she said. "They were all pretending to be the crew to find out what we knew. How did you get away from the rest of them? Hang on, where's Sam? And Jabari and the other guys who were with you?"

"I know about Stella," Lora said. "They turned on us out there, but our guys got the jump on them. Not all of them made it." She looked gratefully at the Guardian and Agent standing protectively nearby. "I was knocked out for a while and by the time I came to, we were halfway here."

Eva silently thanked the universe again for the courageous Guardians and loyal Agents who had done so much for them in the race.

"And Jabari and Sam?"

"Jabari had already gotten out to track Alex but we've lost communication with him too. And Sam . . ." She sighed heavily. "Now I've lost Jabari, Alex *and* Sam."

"No," Eva said, "it's not your fault. I'm sure we'll find him."

They turned when the door of the station opened. A man in an orange snowsuit emerged and rushed to them. Over the wind they could not hear him—but he was pointing at the station, where another crew member stood by the door and waved them inside.

"You're sure there's no sign of Sam?" Lora asked Jedi over the communications link. This one was perfectly clear, unlike the radio and satellite phones that they had brought.

"Sorry, no," Jedi said. "The storm is skirting your location, going out to sea, but it's still enough to wreak havoc on any kind of search."

Eva looked to Gabriella and Arianna, who appeared as worried as she felt.

"But I *have* plotted where Alex may be," Jedi said.

"You have?" Lora asked, hope in her voice.

"Yes," he said.

"Tell us, we'll head there," Eva said.

"It's OK," Jedi replied. "Someone else is on the way to help him. You sit tight and wait for news on Sam. Don't worry—I *will* find him. I'll contact you again soon."

"What did Jedi mean, someone else?" Eva asked anxiously.

"He must mean other Guardians or loyal Agents, such as we have left," Lora said. "I get the impression he didn't want to say on an open line."

"Maybe Jabari!" Arianna said. "Maybe he spoke to Jedi?"

"It would be great to get news of Jabari, I'm very worried about him," Lora replied. "He's a tough man, but this is not exactly his usual terrain."

"And where did you last see Sam?" Eva asked.

"Out there, near the mountains. He was in the snowcat with, I now assume, Stella."

What little color Eva had in her cheeks drained completely.

"Think he's OK?" Gabriella asked carefully.

Lora looked like she was going to cry, but then her cheeks flushed and she stood, angry.

"Lora, it's OK—he'll be OK," Eva said. "He *has* to be."

"He's tough," Arianna said. "Right now, he is probably at some other research outpost."

"Or heading for where Jedi tracked Hans to," Eva said.

"Where is that?" Arianna asked.

"Forty miles northeast of here," Lora said. "The other side of the mountains, towards the coast."

"We can't get there in this weather, can we?" Gabriella said.

"Well, we can't just stay here," Eva said.

"Then we have no choice," Lora said.

SAM

Sam gave up on the GPS. It wasn't working at all. He followed the compass instead, trusting that it would lead him in the right direction and that he'd come to the Chilean station if he stayed on that heading.

The mountains were visible to his left. Behind them, a wall of gray clouds gathered as the storm started to come back around.

Sam moved as fast as he could on foot. The wind was at his back and helped—a lot.

Sometimes, too much.

The crevasses were so large that they were easy to spot. There was no way he could cross one, so he followed the ridges to where they came close together and jumped over the narrowest gaps, which sounded easier than it was. Twice in the first ten minutes, Sam tripped and fell, stopping just in time to avoid rolling down a bottomless crack in the ice. He paced slowly across the uneven ground until he came to a gap that was small enough to leap over, then he would get his bearings again and keep going.

Three miles. Maybe an hour's trek in this weather and with these obstacles.

Sam didn't have time to think more about the journey ahead because at that very moment, the world disappeared.

"Arghh!" Sam leaned back and pulled out his ice ax, spearing it into the ground in one fluid movement. The ax punched through the snow-covered ice and buried itself with a dull sound.

"Arghhhhh!" Sam held on tight as he slipped down the crevasse, slowing, but not fast enough. His gloved grip slipped from the ax.

"*No!*" he yelled, but he didn't fall far—the thin rope around his wrist that tied him to the ice ax held him as he dangled in the cold air.

Man, that was close.

He was not looking forward to the climb back out.

A long, hard hour later, Sam stumbled into the Chilean station, quite literally. He face-planted against the side wall of a building that he couldn't even see for the snow that had drifted against it.

It was empty.

Worse—it had been burned, almost to the ground. Black smoke drifted in the strong wind. He could no longer see the mountains as the weather had swallowed them up.

Who did this . . . ?

"I have an idea who," Sam said to himself, thinking of Solaris. He instinctively looked around, as though he might appear right there, a tall dark figure emerging from the white gloom, but there was nothing but the remains of the base.

He looked back at his footprints and saw shiny bullet casings at his feet. A gunfight had raged here. He looked closer at a burned hut. It was crude, and the fire was not the result of a flame weapon but explosives that had blasted a hole in the wall.

This wasn't Solaris. This was someone else . . .

He walked around, using his ice ax as an anchor in the wind, searching for signs of where they'd cut through the ice.

Find it—and find the way through. Wherever those ruins are, I'm going to bet that's where Hans and Alex are.

Sam stepped forward once more and fell feetfirst into a hole in the ground.

And fell.

And fell.

As he frantically threw out his arms to slow his descent, he made his Stealth Suit expand, feeling it inflate inside his snowsuit as he plummeted down and down . . .

XAVIER

"What is it?" Maria asked, looking up at the ceiling that seemed as large as the night sky and filled with as many stars.

"It's the rock," Dr. Dark said.

"Granite," Phoebe said. "The weight above us is squeezing the quartz crystals in it, creating immense pressure and the result is this glow."

"Like glowworms, or fireflies," Rapha said.

"Earth is a magical place," Poh said with wonder.

"Yeah, I think you're right," Cody muttered, staring at the ceiling.

"This is very like what I saw with Sam," Issey said, "in Japan. A room that glowed. The crystals somehow conducted the electricity—and there was a chair, when Sam sat in it, he completed the circuit."

The others nodded, remembering Issey and Sam's story from their adventure in Tokyo and on Ghost Island.

"There are things about this planet," Dr. Dark said to them all, "that we have no idea about. Not because we don't know it. But because we've forgotten it and it's been hidden from us."

"Dad?" Xavier said. "What about the map? Will the map show us where we need to go?"

Dr. Dark smiled. "There's only one way to find out."

Xavier followed his father through the large water tunnel they now found themselves in. This one certainly predated the Romans—there was no smooth lining on the walls and ceiling, and it was big enough for a bus to drive through. The water was ankle deep in spots. There were stains on the walls that showed at times, long ago, it had been filled to the roof with fast-flowing water.

"This goes under the pyramids?" Xavier asked, walking next to his father.

"In a way," he replied. "Eventually, I should say. Though I didn't bring my GPS with me last time. Big mistake."

"Wait, last time?" Xavier said. "You've been down here this far already, on your own?"

"I, ah . . ." Dr. Dark looked to his son then back at the others who were a few steps behind, the glow of their caving headlamps bobbing up and down as they walked. "The maze?" he said.

"Yeah."

"I went there, two days ago."

"And?"

"And—I got out, this morning."

"Two whole days! You were lost in there for two *days?*" Xavier forced himself not to shout and bring the others' attention to their conversation.

What are we doing down here?

"It's a complicated maze," Dr. Dark explained.

"Did you find anything?" Xavier said.

"Oh, yes, plenty."

"But?"

"But—well, let's say I didn't find what I expected to find. And I can't remember every twist and turn I took in there. My flashlight ran out of power after the first day."

"You . . ." Xavier looked back at the others, then to his father and said in a low voice. "You can't remember?"

Dr. Dark shook his head.

"And you were trapped in the dark all that time?" Xavier said.

"Yes."

"And now you want to go in there again, and take us with you?"

"But I know where I'm going now."

"What?!" Xavier exploded, unable to keep the volume down this time.

"Shhh, you'll make the others nervous."

"*I'm* nervous!" Xavier said quietly, looking back at those

behind them. "How do you know we're not going to get lost again?"

"Trust me, Xavier," Dr. Dark said. He gave Xavier a long, searching look.

"Well," Xavier mumbled. "It's not that I don't want to trust you, Dad, but . . ."

"Please, son."

Xavier was floored to witness his father's vulnerability.

He's asking me for help.

For the first time ever.

"OK, I guess if you're sure you know where you're going."

"I do, I promise," Dr. Dark said. "Look! There it is!"

The water at their feet spread out to a thin film on the floor as they came to another large cavern. Not a natural cave, Xavier could see, from the uniformity of the walls and ceiling carved out of the rock and the square edges all around. Maybe it had been some kind of natural waterway once, and it had been enlarged years later.

Before them was an underground river, a stone bridge crossing it.

"Over there!" Dr. Dark called out, pointing ahead with his flashlight. "That's the way to the maze. We've found it!"

EVA

They drove the snowcat for half an hour and stopped. The engine was on, the heater on full, the gas gauge at half full—good for another few hours at least.

"What is it?" Eva asked.

"The GPS is down," Lora replied, tapping the screen on the dashboard.

"How can the GPS go down?" Arianna asked. "It's a satellite system—it's always working."

"Not if the satellites aren't working." Lora looked at another GPS unit, this one handheld. "Not if they go down."

"How can a satellite 'go down'?" Eva asked.

"If it's destroyed," Lora said.

"Who can do such a thing—destroy a satellite?" Arianna asked. "Surely not Stella, not Solaris? Only a country could do that—a big military, with a missile. Right?"

"I'm not sure about that," Lora said. "I'm not sure what anyone is capable of anymore."

They fell silent, the four of them contemplating this new possibility, this new escalation. The only sounds were the rumble of the huge engine and the whir of the heater.

"Surely no country or government *would* do that?" Eva asked. "Imagine the international uproar if they did."

"But if it's only communication down here in Antarctica that's knocked out, that might be something you could get away with—at least for a while. Who would know?"

"There are not many people here to raise an alarm," Arianna said, looking out the window.

"I doubt it's a nation striking against us," Lora said, her tone changing as though something now made sense. "Since the race went public, the director and the Enterprise have been keeping a close eye on global communication about it, and there was a disturbing amount of corporate interest."

"So you mean big businesses want a piece of the action?" Eva asked.

"It makes sense to me," Lora said. "Some global companies have more money, resources and power than countries. And they're not making money for the good of mankind. They might see the potential in harnessing the Gate's power—"

"Look!" Arianna pointed out the window.

Through the snowdrift, there was movement. Snow bikes—a dozen of them, heading towards them fast.

Lora slammed the 'cat into gear. "I don't know who they are, but we're not getting into a conversation with them out here." She drove the snowcat at full speed but it was not fast enough. Eva looked out the windows and saw that the bikers were not only chasing them, they were catching up.

The snow bikes were the vehicle equivalent of wolves. Up close, they resembled dirt bikes, with big spikes on their wheels. The riders each had guns strapped to their backs, and wore white-and-gray camouflage.

PING! PING! PING!

Bullets hit the snowcat's thick outer skin and ricocheted off.

"They're trying to bully us into stopping," Lora said, her foot flat on the accelerator. "There's little they can do otherwise. This beast weighs a good ten tons and is made of thick steel."

"Well, they're definitely a pest," Eva said. "And while they're out there, we can't stop."

"I know," Lora said.

Eva could see that she was concentrating hard. "Where

are you headed?"

Lora tapped the compass in front of her. "There."

"The US base?"

Lora nodded.

"You know where that is?"

"Not too far at this speed," Lora replied.

"But that's near the last known location we had for Alex, right?" Eva said.

"We can't lead these guys to him, or Sam," Gabriella said.

"But what if we *do*?" Eva said. "Lead them towards Alex, I mean. If he's with Hans, and Stella and her guys are headed there too . . ."

Lora looked up from the controls. "One way or another, we're going to find someone to make these guys think twice."

ALEX

"This way," Alex said.

The room beyond the wall was a vault. It was a room that seemed to hold things from several eras—a small wooden sailboat, barrels of whale oil, an ancient-looking stack of rough-hewn lumber. It was cooler in there, the lava was clearly not near the rock surface under his feet, and there was a cold wind.

"How'd all this *get* here?" Alex wondered as he walked over to a corner of the room.

"Travelers, over time," Hans replied. "Sometimes the ice caves and lava tubes led out to inlets at the sea. They must have found this cavern and left what they needed for future expeditions. Or perhaps they hid things here, hoping to come back later to get them. There—look!"

He pointed ahead, where some light trickled in from a spot in the ceiling.

Alex looked back to the wrecked wall—it had looked exactly like the wall in that cave he'd found out in the snow, near the thermal lake. The realization hit him like a brick.

Those smooth walls sealed off the pyramid complex. The cave I found was just another part of this complex, but I was coming at it from the other side. Now I'm inside.

"It's here," Alex said, pausing by the boat. He looked around it. It could not have sailed here from far—it must have been a lifeboat for another, larger ship. "But I can't remember exactly."

"Spanish, or Portuguese, I'd guess," Ahmed said, closely inspecting the craft. "Fifteenth century, probably—from when they were sending ships to the far reaches of the seas, discovering the world."

"That fits our time frame," Hans said. He pointed to it. "Search it, top to bottom. Tear it apart if you have to," he ordered his men.

To Alex's dismay, the men took to breaking up the boat with gusto.

"You're destroying history!" Ahmed cried out, desperately taking photographs as the men dismantled the boat.

It took them only a few minutes to unearth a wooden chest, which Alex recognized as more of his dream flooded back.

"Wait!" Alex said.

"What is it?" Hans replied, preoccupied with a golden spear that he'd found among a stack of old weaponry.

"I remember!" Alex said, looking around. "My dream— we're not alone!"

"What?" Hans asked.

"I remember standing here, like this, talking about this wooden ship, and then . . ."

"Then?" Hans said. "Who comes? What does it mean?"

"He means," a voice said, "your days of treasure hunting are over."

Alex looked up. Stella stood there, leaning over the edge of the tunnel above, her rogue Agents leering down with her.

"Really?" Hans said, then, quicker than Alex could have believed, he pulled out a grenade, yanked out the pin and flung it upward over the edge of the hole above them.

Alex dived for cover.

BOOM!

Alex coughed, trying not to breathe in the billowing smoke all around them. Dr. Kader was on the ground next to him, frantically crawling away from the blast. Alex went down onto his hands and knees, feeling around in the thick smoke for the chest. He fumbled to open the clasps, the open chest falling from his hands. He heard the Gear tumble out onto the stone with a gentle tink.

He looked up to see the hole above blocked with rocks and debris.

Ha! Take that, Stella.

Now I've just got to keep the Gear away from Hans.

Alex stopped as he felt something.

The Gear!

His fingers wrapped around it and he lifted the palm-sized Gear up close to his face.

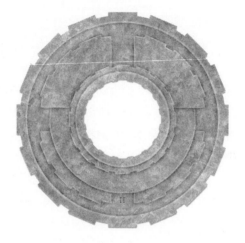

Alex tucked it into his waistband and, taking a deep breath, broke out into a flat-out run.

SAM

Sam saw the grenade go off just before his final fall. From where he'd landed on a huge pile of soft snow, he'd hiked through a tunnel, where there'd been nothing but darkness until he'd spotted Stella and her men. As the explosion ripped through the tunnel, the ground beneath Sam's feet gave way and he fell downward into a large chamber.

When he came to his senses and sat up, he saw Alex, dressed just in his shorts, running towards a light beyond.

Sam sprinted after the fleeing figure of his friend. He skidded to a stop as soon as he ran up a flight of stairs. The heat was overwhelming.

Is that lava?

Is this a pyramid?

What the—?

Sam turned to gaze up.

"Sam!" Alex called. "Over here! Up here, quick!"

Sam ran up the pyramid steps, unzipping his snowsuit as he did so and as he reached the top platform of the pyramid, he ditched it.

"Finally! It's great to see you!" Sam said, the dream forgotten. He put out a hand to Alex.

Alex ignored it. Instead, he grabbed Sam and hugged him tight.

"I'm glad you're OK," Alex said.

"Me too," Sam said. "And that you're still my friend—I mean, in my dream, I wasn't sure. I thought you might have really sided with Hans."

"Yeah," Alex said letting Sam go. "I was just faking him out. I got here and got the Gear, didn't I?"

"You sure did, buddy."

"It's been so long since we were together," Alex said.

"I know, and so much has happened. It's hard to know where to even—" Sam began.

A muffled explosion rang out and lava bubbled up from a new fissure that was breaking apart in the rock floor.

"Let's talk later, we need another way out!" Sam yelled.

"I know one. Being the person with the Gear dream has to have some advantages, right?"

"Fine with me—" Sam stopped as he heard a whistling noise.

Alex looked to Sam. Sam pulled him to the ground, just in time.

WHOOSH!

A jet of fire whizzed past them.

KLAP-BOOM!

The explosion echoed throughout the entire chamber,

raining rocks and chucks of ice all around, a fierce hailstorm inside the cavern.

"What—what was that?" Alex yelled.

"Rocket launcher," Sam replied, looking in the direction it had been fired from. "I remember the sound, from New York. And it was fired by the same person who did it last time," Sam said. "Stella."

"But she won't kill us, right?"

"No, not yet," Sam said. "But she reckons she's so good that she misses on purpose."

"Huh?"

"She's not shooting to kill us, she's corralling us. She wants us to head in some other direction."

"What's in that direction?"

"Probably a trap—her guys waiting for us or whatever."

"OK, well, follow me!" Alex yelled as another whistle filled the air.

Sam followed close behind. The heat was intense. They ran around the pyramid and down the steps at the other side, and skidded to a stop.

A tall figure stood in front of them, emerging slowly from the shadows.

"Sam!" Alex said, shoving him away. "*Run!*"

"It's OK!" Sam said. "It's not Solaris!"

The tall figure emerged. It was Jabari. His Stealth Suit was charred and smoldering—he'd clearly had a close call, either with a missile or some lava.

And he had a gun in his hands. It was pointed at Alex.

"Jabari? What are you *doing?*" Sam shouted.

Jabari came closer, silent. The gun remained trained on Alex.

"It's OK," Sam said, moving towards him, his arms outstretched to reassure him. "Alex is on *our* side! We've got the Gear. Let's get out of here!"

"I don't think that your new friend is on *our* side, Sam," Alex muttered.

Jabari nodded, smiling slowly.

"We . . . the Egyptian Guardians are sworn to protect the Dream Gate, Sam," he said, unsteady on his feet, the gun wavering at Alex. "*Not* Dreamers."

He's injured.

"But . . ." Sam paused. "You're not going to let us finish the race?"

Jabari shook his head. "Sorry, Sam. I liked you. I really did."

"You traitor!" Sam said. "You said you'd realized you were on the wrong path!"

Jabari nodded. "I did, but that was a lie, Sam. If only you had not survived the helicopter crash in the first place. This could have ended there and then."

"*What!*" Alex's mind was clearly reeling to catch up with current events. "This guy tried to *kill* us and you thought he was on our side?"

"He admitted it," Sam said. "Said the Egyptian Guardians had a change of heart, were going to protect us."

"It was more a change of *tactics*," Jabari said. "I thought I'd see if you could get to the end, to the Gate, then I'd do what had to be done and bury the secret all over again."

"Why?"

"The Dream Gate is too much power. It allowed my ancestors, the ancient Egyptians, to rule the world for centuries. There's a reason it has been buried since. Some . . . " Jabari stumbled, unsteady on his feet, but he righted himself against the wall. The gun was steady in his grip.

Sam tried to catch Alex's eye.

We have to rush him. Find a moment when he's weakest.

"Maybe the Gate is destined to be found," Sam said, defiant. "If not by us, perhaps by another 13 one day—a hundred years, a thousand years from now."

"Maybe," Jabari said. "But we will be even more ready."

"I don't think so," a deep voice said.

They all turned in surprise to see another figure emerging from the shadows.

"Professor?"

"Jabari, put the gun down," the Professor commanded. In his hand he held a small pistol, pointed straight at the leader of the Egyptian Guard.

Nothing happened for a moment. Stalemate. Sam and Alex stood still, barely breathing, watching. The Professor didn't move. Jabari was swaying slightly on his feet.

He might pass out any second.

Jabari moved fast—he turned his gun around to fire at the Professor.

A shot rang out.

Jabari fell.

In the stunned silence, Sam looked from the fallen body of Jabari to the Professor. The pistol was smoking from the barrel.

"Oh, *man!*" Alex gasped. "It's *really* good to see you, Professor!"

"Likewise, I'm sure, Alex," the Professor said. "Now, I think we can all agree it is well and truly time to leave this place."

"**W**ait!" A voice shouted. "Wait!"

"Who is it?" Sam said, looking around. He rushed to Dr. Kader, who was dazed and lying on the ground. Sam and the Professor helped the Egyptologist to his feet.

"Wait!" The voice was actually coming from below their position, from a huge crack in the ground.

"Hold on!" Alex yelled. He got onto his stomach, looking down a fissure that was glowing red with heat. Sam could see Hans trapped down there on a ledge. He hadn't fallen in—he'd *climbed* in to get the golden spear, which lay on another ledge below where he stood.

"Leave it, Hans!" Alex yelled. "Climb up, you have to come now!"

"Alex!" Sam shouted. Bits of stone began to fall from the ceiling of the cavern as the lava shifted and moved inside the dormant volcano. "We have to get out of here."

Alex looked at Sam and the Professor and shook his head.

"We have our own race to win!" Sam said. "Come on!"

"We can help him," Alex said.

"He's too far down, we can't reach him. Alex—it's us or him," Sam said. "There's no time!"

Alex looked from Sam to Hans, who was still reaching for the spear.

"I'll just be one more minute," Hans called up. "Wait for me, Alex."

Sam ran towards his friend. Explosions from the volcano echoed around them. Debris rained down. Fire and brimstone.

"Alex . . ."

Alex looked up at Sam.

"It's time to go, you can't save him if he doesn't want to be saved." He pulled at Alex's sleeve. "Come on!"

Alex looked down at Hans, edging towards the spear. "He's not all bad, you know."

"Don't let Hans fool you, Alex," Sam said, his voice quiet. "He's not your friend, no matter what he's said or what you think. He sold you lies—he wants your Gear. He wants the Bakhu machine for himself."

"I know, I know you're right!" Alex said, looking Sam in the eye. "But it seems wrong to abandon him now, after all this time together."

Sam could see that his friend was conflicted.

Alex turned back to look down at Hans. "Let it go!" he screamed to him.

Hans would not listen. He was on the tiny ledge below now, crawling along it and getting closer to the golden spear.

"I am nearly there, Alex," Hans said. "So close . . . I can get it. I can have it all. This, the machine, all of it!"

Sam could see that the ground they were standing on was crumbling. Every second, more stone fell away. In ten seconds, it'd be gone.

"Alex!" Sam said. "Quick—come back from the edge, the whole thing's going to go!"

Another explosion echoed through the chamber and large rocks cascaded down. A deep rumble echoed through the volcano.

"If we don't leave now," Sam said, wincing in pain as a falling rock hit his arm, "it's *over*. This whole race. You and me, everything—finished. Do you understand?"

Alex nodded, pulling back from the edge, even as he kept his eyes on Hans.

More explosions rang out and a red river of lava broke through the rock wall and cut the site in two.

As they came away from the edge, they were blown off their feet—an explosion soaring up from inside the crevasse, lava already spilling up over the edge.

"No!" Alex yelled.

"He's *gone!*" Sam said. "Let's get out of here!"

The two of them ran. Sam glanced back. The lava was at their heels.

"We'll have to jump!" Alex shouted.

Sam looked ahead, to where the Professor and Dr. Kader were standing.

We'll have to jump over the lava—it's a big jump.

"Faster!" Sam said, overtaking Alex at a sprint, hitting the edge of the crack and leaping. His arms and legs kept spinning as he flew through the air. Alex was next to him. The heat from the molten stone rose up and stung his face.

We're going to make it!

Sam landed with one foot on the far edge of the crevasse and shifted his weight forward. Alex landed in a tumble, getting to his feet.

"That was—" Alex said.

Sam started to fall—the ground under his foot crumbled away and he dropped like a stone.

But he didn't drop into the lava. He stopped, as though in midair.

"I've got you, Sam!" Alex said. He was on the ground with both hands gripping tight on to Sam's arms.

"Thanks," Sam said, stunned at the sight of the lava thirty feet below his feet. Sensing movement behind him, he turned to see the lava spilling over the edge forming a super-hot waterfall. "Get me up!"

"I'm trying!"

"Here!" A new voice said. "Quickly!"

Sam looked up—Lora was there, next to Alex, and together they hauled Sam up.

"Come on," Lora said, pushing them along. "This place is going to blow!"

Outside, a huge, bright-yellow truck with tank treads and large stenciled letters proclaiming *Amundsen-Scott Station—USA* was waiting for them. Sam and Lora piled in after the Professor and Dr. Kader. Alex paused at the door and looked back at the mountain that was becoming a volcano right before their eyes, then climbed aboard.

"The others?" Sam asked. "Eva and Gabriella and Arianna?"

"They're all fine," Lora said. "I left them at the US station—it's safe there. We were chased by some guys on bikes, we still don't know who they were, but once we made it to the base, they disappeared."

Sam nodded and stared out the window.

"We've got the Gear," Alex said. "That's what counts, right?"

Lora nodded, smiling.

"No sign of Solaris?" Sam asked.

"No," the Professor said.

"And the others?" Sam asked. "The rest of the last 13?"

"They're in Egypt, with Dr. Dark," the Professor replied. "Your mother's there too," he said to Alex. "She's been worried about you. You must call her as soon as you can."

"What are they doing there?" Alex asked.

"Lying low at Dr. Kader's workshop," the Professor said, "and waiting for us. We'll get there soon enough."

"I suspect," Dr. Kader said, "that Dark and your friends are having a good dig through my papers and research, looking for clues about the location of Bakhu."

"Bakhu?" Sam asked. "Stella mentioned it too. So it's also a place? But how do we know we need to go there? To Egypt, I mean."

"Bakhu," the Professor replied, "*is* the name of a place, Sam. But most believe it is more of a legend or myth. It is the mountain from which the sun rises, giving birth to the day."

Sam remembered the sunset from his dreams before, how it had been comforting. He couldn't remember a dream about the sun rising.

"And the machine was named after it?" Alex asked.

"We now believe so, yes," the Professor replied.

"It does kinda make sense now . . ." Sam said, looking at the key that dangled from around his neck.

"What does?" Alex asked.

"That this all ends in Egypt," Sam replied, looking at the hieroglyphics cut into the key, which he now knew spelled out the word "thirteen." "It started there, with this key—inside the Star of Egypt. Remember? I went to the pyramids and I didn't know why. It's like I went there because I had to."

Sam paused, looking out the thick glass window of the truck as they rumbled up to the American station. The volcano behind them erupted with an earsplitting bang.

Bright-red and orange lava spewed from the top, dark smoke battling the white snowy winds of the super storm. "Us going to Egypt? It's like we're going home."

37

XAVIER

"I can make that," Xavier said, looking across the gap.

"Dream on," Cody said, standing next to him. The missing chunk of floor, just in front of the maze entrance was just a bit too big to jump.

"That gap wasn't there before," Dr. Dark muttered. "How strange."

"You don't think I can make it?"

"I know you can't," Cody said, crossing his arms.

Xavier looked at him, standing there.

Right.

"Fine," Xavier said, pacing away. "Stand back."

"Xavier, no!" Poh said.

"I'll be fine," Xavier replied. "Just keep back, I need a run-up."

Phoebe caught his arm as he unspooled the rope.

"Xavier, you don't have to do this," she said. "We can get the Agents standing guard up at Dr. Kader's workshop to come down and help us."

"Actually, I'm not feeling so great," Zara piped up, stepping forward. "The darkness, I find it . . ."

"I can take her back to the workshop," Issey volunteered. "She needs fresh air, I think."

"Thank you," Zara said, looking relieved and leaning on Issey as she took deep breaths.

"Sure, that's a good idea," Phoebe said. "I'd better—I'd like to stay with everyone else." Her eyes flicked to Dr. Dark and Xavier could see she was anxious not to leave them down there alone with him.

In case he really does flip out.

"We'll see you guys later, OK?" Issey said. "Stay safe and we'll send down the Agents with equipment for you." He and Zara started walking back as the others called out their good-byes.

"And who knows what we might find on the other side," Rapha said. "Maybe it's better to wait anyway."

Xavier shook his head, handing an end of the rope to Phoebe.

"Why delay?" he said, tying the other end of rope around his waist. "Besides, this is a walk in the park."

Xavier looked over to his father, who was smiling like he was enjoying the show—that what his son was about to do was something to marvel at and be proud of.

At least one of us is confident.

"Good luck," Maria said to him.

Xavier nodded. His father gave him a thumbs-up.

Great, my dad's lost his marbles from lack of sleep, and I . . . I can do this.

Xavier closed his eyes and took a couple of deep breaths.

It's only a jump. Think of it as the long jump on field day. Piece of cake.

He opened his eyes and ran faster than he ever had before.

And jumped.

"That was cool, man!" Cody said to Xavier. Cody high-fived him as Xavier grinned. They waited as the others followed Cody across on the rope.

"This way," Dr. Dark said, consulting the map. "This is the way I should have come in the first place. Not long now."

Xavier watched as his father led them into the maze, side tunnels shooting off in each direction.

"For what it's worth," Cody said, walking next to Xavier, "I'm sorry for what I said about your father. He's not crazy."

"Ha!" Xavier laughed. "Cody, don't apologize for that. Right now, I think he *is* a little nuts. So long as he doesn't get us lost."

Xavier looked ahead to see his father a little off in front, shaking his head and muttering to himself.

"Um, guys," Xavier said, "can you give me a minute with my dad?"

The others nodded and waited patiently as Xavier approached his father. As he came closer to him, Dr. Dark moved further away, disappearing around a corner.

Xavier jogged to catch up to him. "Dad? Where are you going?"

Dr. Dark turned around.

"Dad—what's happening? What aren't you telling me?"

"Xavier . . ." Dr. Dark's voice trailed off.

"What? You're worrying me. Are my friends going to be OK down here?"

"Yes, they will be."

"Tell me what's going on, *please.*"

Xavier could see his father looked conflicted.

What is it? What's so hard for him to tell me?

"This race," Dr. Dark said, sitting down, "it's about to end."

Xavier sat next to his father. "I know that."

"You don't know it all," Dr. Dark said. "You don't know the half of it."

"Then tell me," Xavier said. "I'm listening and I want to know."

Dr. Dark looked to his son. "It's about Solaris."

"What about him?"

"He's . . . he's . . ."

A deep metallic voice came out of the darkness.

"I'm right here."